For Forester

J. NATHAN

Edited by Stephanie Elliot

Cover Design by Letitia at RBA Designs
Cover Photo by Lindee Robinson
Cover Models Jeff Kline and Becca Schnyders

Manufactured in the United States of America

First Edition July 2017

PROLOGUE

Charles loved the Mercury Hotel. At least it would seem that way given his weekly business meetings there, missing dinner on multiple occasions. And though I'd never been invited along, I always admired its beautiful exterior, with its old brick architecture and tall windows. But as I sped through the streets of downtown Alabama in a pretty black dress, I knew I'd be there soon, surprising Charles with a fortieth birthday party.

CJ sat in his booster seat in the backseat in khakis and a light green button-down that matched his eyes. Getting a five-year-old to dress in anything other than sweats and a T-shirt was a miracle, but we were getting there early to decorate for his dad's party where a hundred of Charles' closest friends and associates would be celebrating with us.

I parked in front of the vast steps, leaving my car packed with boxes of decorations and favors for the bellhop to help with.

CJ and I raced up the steps and laughed our way through the revolving front door until we'd stepped into the lobby with all its fancy mirrors and elaborate fountains. My heels clicked on the marble floor as we approached the receptionist where I asked for

Marianne, the hotel's event planner. We'd never met in person, planning the entire party over the phone. But she'd asked me to meet her at three o'clock so she could assist with all the last-minute preparations before the guests arrived at seven.

While the receptionist paged her, CJ and I took in the beautiful space around us. From the indoor waterfall to the glass elevator, the place was exquisite. Charles was a partner at a law firm which footed the bills for his meetings here. And I could see why clients would be impressed.

"Hey, Daddy's here," CJ said, tugging on my hand.

I gasped as I tugged CJ around the receptionist's counter so we wouldn't spoil the surprise.

But why was he four hours early?

Twisting deep in my stomach told me something wasn't right. Told me I needed to look. Told me I needed to see it with my own two eyes.

I peeked around the desk, catching sight of Charles stepping into the elevator with his hand clutching the hand of a beautiful young redhead. I blinked hard, ensuring my eyes weren't playing tricks on me. Vomit crept up the back of my throat as Charles turned and wrapped his arms around the woman, pressing his lips to hers.

I fought to catch my breath as I watched in horror as my husband kissed another woman.

I needed to sit, to breathe, to think.

I turned on unsteady legs and rushed CJ out the revolving door. The fresh February air hit as soon as I stepped outside, dropping down in the middle of the front steps on the verge of a nervous breakdown.

CJ dropped down next to me. "Mom? Are you okay?"

I pulled in another breath as my limbs trembled wildly. "I don't know." This was what it felt like to have my world ripped out from beneath me. To know I did everything for a man who could have cared less about destroying his family. To wish someone dead.

"What was Daddy doing in there?" CJ's voice echoed through my frazzled brain, a clear reminder that I needed to pull it together—even though all I really wanted to do was rip out the redhead's extensions and claw out Charles' eyeballs.

But I was a twenty-nine-year-old woman with a son. I was better than that.

"I don't know, sweetie." Instead of sitting there basking in self-pity, I grabbed my phone and dialed, shakily lifting it to my ear. "Hi Marianne. No. I actually had to leave. I wasn't feeling well. Could you do me a favor? Could you make it an open bar tonight instead of the cash bar we decided on? Also, let me give you the new credit card I want everything charged to."

With trembling hands, I managed to pull Charles' business credit card from my clutch without dropping it. I read off the card number with the slightest bit of satisfaction that I actually had his card on me. It was only for emergencies. But I'd say having a cheating husband who just went and destroyed his family constituted an emergency.

I left the hotel and dropped CJ at my parents. Luckily, he didn't bombard me with too many questions about why we were skipping his dad's party. From there, I called my cousin Jerry, the only lawyer I knew who wasn't Charles' coworker or friend. He advised me to visit the bank and open an account in my name, which I did, transferring half our savings into it. My name was on the account, therefore, I had the legal right to do whatever I pleased with it.

And that night, while Charles celebrated with his friends, including the redhead from the elevator, a locksmith changed the locks on our house while I packed up Charles' belongings and left them on the front lawn. Then I switched off my phone and stayed at my parents' house until I was sure he was gone.

And hopefully out of our lives forever.

CHAPTER ONE
Three Months Later

Marin

I reached behind me, grabbing for the bag of cheddar goldfish from the floor of the backseat, desperately needing a snack. Yup. That's what my life had come to. Eating stale goldfish off the floor of my car. If my college friends could see me now.

I'd dropped CJ off at camp and had a few hours to clean the house that had suddenly gone to hell and search the Internet for a job. I pulled into my neighborhood, passing all the fancy homes with their brick fronts, fancy stained-glass doors, and meticulously manicured lawns. The same ones that had drawn Charles and me to this neighborhood seven years ago. I remember imagining our future there. Imagining Charles surprising me with breakfast on Saturday mornings. Twirling me around the kitchen to our favorite song. Our laughter filling our beautiful new space.

At twenty-two, I was such a fool.

Scratch that. At twenty-nine, I was still a fool.

Those days had never happened. My marriage had been a sham. Something I was part of, but never really in. I'd merely been playing a part. I never saw what was going on. Never saw I was the only one invested.

I turned from the houses that lined the street. A basketball bounced out in front of my car. I hit the brakes. A man jogged out in front of my car, bending to grab it. When he stood back up, he turned toward me and flashed a wide smile. Two dimples dug into the sides of his mouth, sending my mind reeling. I recognized those dimples. They belonged to Trace Forester, the neighborhood kid who zipped by on his skateboard always smiling and waving as he passed by. That was well before CJ. That was when I'd just graduated with my Bachelor's and had nothing to fill my days but homework from my grad classes. Now those dimples belonged to a man. At least he looked like a man, all six foot something and ripped. His white shirt gripped massive arms and his dark hair was now cleanly cut and not shaggy like the little skateboarder years before. And though the blue eyes that were currently staring at me were the same, the face with its square jaw covered in a dusting of stubble had matured.

Trace walked around to the side of my car. I lowered the country music on my radio and dusted the goldfish crumbs off the front of my shirt. I turned toward my open window with a smile that hopefully said I wasn't trying too hard to look put together when my world had recently fallen apart. No doubt he knew. His mother was the biggest gossip in town.

"Hey," he said, ducking his head to look in the car window. "I haven't seen you in a while."

I smiled. "Yeah." I couldn't stop my eyes from drifting over his chest, especially with his shirt stretched across it. "Last time I saw you, you were skateboarding around here like a maniac." Realizing I might've been staring a little too long, my eyes jumped to his.

"I haven't skateboarded since junior high." He ran a hand through his dark hair with an amused laugh. "You do realize I'm a senior in college, right?"

I laughed to myself, unable to recall the last time I'd actually seen him. Once CJ was born, my life became hectic, my mind oftentimes distracted. Probably the reason I didn't know my husband was cheating on me. "Sorry. I guess life happened."

"Yeah. I heard you had a kid."

I nodded. "CJ. He's five. He kind of reminds me of you when you were younger."

His brows lifted. "Wild?"

I snickered. "Happy."

His eyes lingered on mine longer than what was probably acceptable given our substantial age difference.

"So." I cleared my throat to break the sudden awkwardness. "How do you like college?"

He smirked. "It's treating me all right."

I suddenly felt like I'd missed something. "Why do I get the feeling you're laughing at me?"

He shook his head slowly, his eyes remaining on mine. "I'm not laughing."

"Then what don't I understand?"

"I'm Alabama's number one receiver."

My eyes rounded. "Sorry. I should probably know that, shouldn't I?"

"I'm surprised my mother hasn't told you."

I shrugged. "I kind of keep to myself these days."

"Yeah. I heard you're getting divorced."

My eyes flashed down. Did people think I hadn't been a good enough wife? A good enough mother?

"Never liked the guy," he admitted matter-of-factly.

My eyes shot back to his. "No?"

He scoffed. "Hell, no. The guy seemed like a total douche."

I threw back my head and laughed, feeling a giant weight lift off my shoulders. If Trace knew the truth about Charles, and he'd been away at school, hopefully the rest of the neighborhood did, too. "So, what are you up to this summer?" I asked.

He shrugged. "Working out so I'm ready for the season, and making some cash. You know Lou's Beach Bar?"

"Do I?" I laughed, shaking my head at the wild recollections flooding my brain. "My friends and I practically lived there when we were in college…God. That was so long ago."

"Yeah. Cuz you're so old."

"That was another life."

"You're getting a divorce. Your life didn't end," he said, so nonchalant—so sure—I almost believed him. "Why'd you ask what I was doing this summer?"

I swallowed. *Me and my big mouth.* "I might have a proposition for you."

He quirked his brow. "I like where this is going."

Gah. His confidence was off the charts. "I need a guy around."

"You don't say?"

Oh shit. "For CJ," I quickly added. "Camp ends soon and I need someone to spend some time with him. You know, play catch or something. His father never really takes the time to do that when he sees him. I don't want him to be an awkward, uncoordinated kid."

"Yeah. That would suck."

"Well?" I said. "You up for the challenge?"

Trace's eyes zoned in on mine. "I'm always up for a challenge."

For some reason, I got the feeling he wasn't talking about CJ.

"When do you want me to stop by?" he asked.

"Oh. Whenever you can. Just text me. Do you have your phone on you?"

He slipped his hand into the pocket of his basketball shorts.

My eyes followed his hand, noticing the way his shorts hung low on his hips as he pulled the phone from his pocket. Geez. He even had definition there.

Trace cleared his throat.

My eyes jumped to his, my cheeks pulsing with heat. What the hell was wrong with me?

He wore a slight grin, as if amused by the dirty cougar checking him out. "What is it?"

I rattled off my number and he punched it in. I finished by saying, "Marin."

He glanced up at me. "You don't think I know your name?"

I shrugged. "Most kids don't pay attention to stuff like that."

"I'm not a kid," he said, his voice dropping to a lower tenor. "And I did pay attention."

A ripple rolled through my stomach. A dangerous, unexpected ripple. I needed to get the hell out of there. He was a kid for Christ's sake. And he clearly wasn't looking at me the way my body was leading me to believe he was. I was damaged goods. I couldn't even keep a husband. "Well, just text me when you're around," I said off-handedly, so not to appear desperate. "I'll make sure CJ and I are home."

He nodded, stepping back from the car.

"I really appreciate this."

"Not a problem, Marin."

The smooth way my name rolled off his tongue told me I needed to be careful when it came to Trace Forester. He was a kid. And I was a lonely, twenty-nine-year-old, single mother. Things like that were only glamorized on television with housewives and their landscapers, not in real life.

As I pulled away, I glanced in the rearview mirror. Trace stood with his arms folded across his chest watching me go.

CHAPTER TWO

Marin

I puttered around my kitchen, looking for something to occupy my time, but I found myself drawn to the window where I had a clear view of Trace and CJ tossing a football in the backyard. Trace had texted earlier. I never expected him to show up fifteen minutes later. But he had, and I hadn't seen CJ smile that much in a very long time. Sure, he and I had fun together. But there was just something about a boy and a big strong guy who could teach him a thing or two about football that felt right.

My phone rang. I jumped, the guilt of enjoying the view so much startling me. I grabbed the phone from the table. It was my best friend Gayle. "Hey."

"You sleep with him yet?" she asked.

"Oh my God. What is wrong with you?"

"Me? Have you seen the guy in his uniform? The guy could be a freakin' model."

Outside, Trace tossed the football gently so CJ had a slight chance of actually catching it. He didn't. It bounced off the grass in front of him, but he ran after it, laughing as he did. "Yes, I've seen the teenager in my backyard."

"He's not a teenager," Gayle said.

"Yes, he is. I looked it up. He's nineteen."

There was a pause on her end, like she just realized I was a sicko who'd actually looked him up. "Wait. How is he nineteen and a senior?"

"I have no idea."

"Well, who cares?" she said. "You're single and he's hot."

I laughed as I turned from the window and moved into the living room.

"And when are you ever gonna have a hot piece of ass under your roof again?" Gayle asked.

I scoffed. "You're acting like he sees me as anything other than a woman with a kid who needs a guy around."

"Marin, you're beautiful and fun. You deserve to get some action."

"You do realize you're encouraging me to jump his bones, right?"

"I never said jump his bones. Just wear something tight. Bend over and let him see your hot ass. You'd barely have to do anything."

"You're insane." I laughed. "And I could go to jail."

"Why could you go to jail?" a deep voice asked from behind me.

I spun around, my heart drumming in my chest. Trace stood in the doorway smirking, like he'd heard my conversation.

Had he?

"Gayle, I gotta go." I disconnected the call. "Where's CJ?" I was going for nonchalance, but the heat flaming in my cheeks said otherwise.

"He just needed the bathroom. Figured I'd grab him a drink."

I blinked hard as the heat from my cheeks spread to the rest of my body. I hurried into the kitchen and grabbed two bottles of water from the refrigerator. Even Charles wouldn't have thought to grab CJ a drink.

Trace followed me into the kitchen. "So, you didn't say." His deep voice sent chills to parts of my body that had lain dormant for far too long. "Why are you going to jail?"

"Oh, that was just my friend being crazy."

I handed him one of the bottles. His fingertips skimmed mine. My eyes shot to his, but he just smiled like it had been unintentional. Maybe it had been. Maybe all Gayle's talk about bending over was making me jittery. Making me see things that weren't there.

"CJ's a great kid," Trace said.

I stepped back a couple feet, distancing myself from his nearness which was overwhelming now that we stood alone in my kitchen. "Thanks."

"No, I'm serious. He's funny and really athletic."

"He gets that from me," I joked.

"Hey, Trace?" CJ said, bouncing into the kitchen.

Trace turned to him. "What's up, buddy?"

"Can we play basketball tomorrow?"

"Oh, CJ," I said. "Trace is busy. He can't play with you every day."

"Sure I can," Trace said.

My eyes cut to his. "You don't have to do that."

"Maybe I want to."

Do not read into this, Marin. Do not put expectations on him. "When you have time."

"I'll make time," he assured me.

I turned away from him before I did something crazy like hug him for being so much better than Charles.

"Can we Trace?" CJ asked.

"Sure. I'll come get you so we can play on my net." He looked to me. "Is that okay?"

I did one of those shrug-nods that were only acceptable when you were at a total loss for the appropriate words.

He looked to CJ. "Have your basketball ready."

"Okay," CJ said, his eyes all dreamy like Trace hung the moon.

Trace held out his fist which CJ gladly bumped. "See you tomorrow, buddy." He glanced over his shoulder at me. "Bye, Marin."

"Wait." I grabbed my handbag from the counter. "Let me give you something."

Trace took the two steps necessary for his long stride to cross my kitchen. His hand covered mine, stopping me from reaching for my wallet. "Stop."

My heartbeat did a crazy skip, the unexpected strength of his grip and warmth of his touch catching me off guard. "But I—"

He leveled me with serious eyes, lowering his voice so CJ couldn't hear. "I want to be here."

I cocked my head, trying to ignore the tingling of his touch. "I know you're busy."

"Then make me a meal."

"What?"

"Feed me." He released my hand and stepped back. "My mother's cooking sucks."

I stared dumbstruck. One, because his mother still made him meals. And two, because I couldn't believe he actually wanted to spend time with a single mother and her kid when he could be off sweeping girls off their feet with a mere glance.

"Can you do that?" he asked.

"Cook?"

His lips tipped up in the corners. "Make me a meal."

"I can do that."

"I bet there's a lot you can do," he murmured as he walked to the front door.

What the what?

"See you guys," he called before slipping out the door as if he'd never been there at all.

I leaned back against the counter. The knocking of my pulse told me he definitely *had* been there.

"What's wrong, Mom?"

I looked to CJ, his blond hair so much like mine. His green eyes his father's. "Nothing, buddy. Nothing at all."

And this time I wasn't lying to my son.

CHAPTER THREE

Marin

"You coming?" Trace asked the following day before taking CJ to play basketball.

From my spot in the open doorway, I looked at them standing on the front lawn. CJ was so tiny next to Trace's tall frame. But he looked so damn happy. "Me?"

Trace nodded. "Yeah, you."

"Why?"

"Because it's fun." He placed his big hand down on CJ's shoulder, earning him a huge grin from his biggest fan. "And because my buddy here likely has some mad skills he wants to show off in front of his mom."

I smiled, appreciating how he knew just what to say to make CJ worship him even more than he already did. "Maybe I'll come by later. I need to cut the lawn."

His brows shot up. "Cut the lawn?"

I nodded. "Had to get rid of the landscaper."

Trace's brows leveled out, the state of my financial situation obviously hitting him. "Let me do it for you."

I shook my head. "Absolutely not."

"Why not?"

"Because I'm quite capable of pushing a lawnmower."

He stood silently for a long minute. "Fine. But come by after."

"Okay," I relented.

"Good."

"Good," I echoed as they disappeared around the corner toward his house. I wondered what he meant by good. *Good* I was going to see my son play basketball. Or *good* he wanted me there.

God, what was wrong with me? I was a grown woman getting excited over a teenager. *A teenager for Christ's sake.* I was sick. I needed help. Maybe I needed to talk to someone. And I didn't mean Gayle.

I spent the hour after they left mowing the lawn and it was a lot bigger than I realized. I'd let the landscaper go last week and it had been some time since I'd pushed a lawnmower. But I'd done it, and a small sense of accomplishment swept over me. I didn't need Charles. I was getting along just fine without a man in my life. And even if I hadn't found a job yet, I was still managing.

After a quick shower, I whipped up sloppy Joes—something Charles hated—and headed to Trace's house. I stopped behind my neighbor's small hedge and watched them undetected.

CJ ran around Trace's driveway laughing hysterically as he tried unsuccessfully to steal the ball away from Trace. After a couple minutes of teasing him, Trace let him steal the ball, feigning disappointment when CJ shot the ball. His shot didn't even make it halfway to the net, but Trace clapped as he jogged to grab it. "Good one, buddy."

I walked toward them, unable to contain my smile. "Nice shot."

They both twisted, smiling as soon as they spotted me.

"Did you see it?" CJ asked.

"Yep. You almost had him."

"He did," Trace agreed, shooting me a conspiratorial grin. "Gave me a real run for my money. You wanna try?"

I rolled my eyes. "Me?"

"You do realize you answer every one of my questions with a question, right?"

"I do?"

He nodded, smirking at yet another question.

"Well, I'm more of a spectator. I haven't played a sport since high school."

"What'd you play?"

"Volleyball."

"Yeah." His eyes dropped to my legs. The heat his stare elicited had me questioning my favorite cutoffs. "I can see that."

Gahhhh.

Trace grabbed hold of CJ who laughed as he lifted him onto his shoulders. Given Trace's height, CJ would have no trouble dunking the ball. "Come on Mom," CJ called. "Come block me."

Surprising them both, I threw my arms in the air and tried blocking CJ who held the ball on Trace's shoulders. Trace gripped CJ's legs before he moved right. Doing my best to block him, I moved right. Trace moved them left. CJ snort-laughed, igniting laughter in all of us as I followed them to the left.

I couldn't ignore the comfortable feeling that swept over me. This was how easy life should have been. The fun. The laughter. The focus on our child. How did some college guy get that and not Charles? Was it just that he fell out of love with me? Was it that life became too tough when we had responsibilities? Or could life really be this easy?

CJ shot the ball over me and it swished through the net. He howled with excitement as Trace lowered him to the ground and bumped his fist. "Thanks, Trace." CJ turned and threw himself into my arms. "I did it."

I squeezed him into a hug and savored the moment, knowing I'd soon be replaced with friends and school and girls. *Girls.* The dreaded word for all mothers of sons. Especially when that son thought you were the most amazing girl in the world.

"Put me on *your* shoulders, Mom."

I threw back my head in laughter. "Yeah right. You'll crush me."

He stepped out of my arms and looked me up and down. "You're right. I am pretty strong."

My eyes ventured to Trace, standing nearby with his arms crossed and his focus on me.

A smirk slipped across his lips, and I felt fairly confident it was the same one that melted panties on campus. "I'd like a shot."

"*You'd* definitely crush me," I assured him.

He laughed. "That's not what I meant."

I felt the creases in my forehead deepen. "You want me on your shoulders?"

"That'd be interesting," he mused. "But I meant one on one. You and me." He grabbed the ball from the driveway and alternated between hands, bouncing it in front of me, his eyes never wavering from mine. "Scared?" he asked.

"Of what?" I asked.

"Losing."

"Nope. Losing I've mastered. It's winning I need a shot at." I swiped the ball away from him, dribbling it to the far end of the driveway. His deep laughter carried over my shoulders, and soon I felt his body behind me, his arms playfully reaching for the ball. His chest brushed my back slightly, but he kept himself from stealing the ball. I dribbled around him and shot an easy layup which dropped into the net as if I actually knew what I was doing.

CJ cheered and Trace shot me a satisfied grin. He let me make the shot. He let me look good in front of my son. Was there anything he didn't do right?

Happiness swelled inside me. True happiness. I just wished a teenager wasn't making me feel that way.

"I'm hungry," CJ announced.

I looked between the two of them. "I hope you both are. I made sloppy Joe's."

Traces eyes rounded. "I'm invited?"

"A deal's a deal. Unless, you have plans."

A hot as hell smile swept across his lips. "I do now."

* * *

CJ wiped his mouth with his crumpled napkin as he pushed his chair back from the kitchen table. "Enough grown up talk. Can I play a video game?"

"Go ahead," I said.

"I'm a grown up?" Trace asked.

I stood, grabbing the empty dishes. "It happens faster than you know."

"Not for me," CJ said, jumping to his feet and running out of the kitchen. "Love you more than the universe, Mom," he called as his footsteps clomped up the hardwood steps.

"Love you too," I called before looking to Trace. "That. That right there. That's what makes every day worth it. That unconventional love and honesty you'll only ever get from a child."

"I don't think that's only reserved for kids," Trace challenged, standing and grabbing our empty glasses.

I scoffed. "Haven't met many who I can trust wholeheartedly."

He took the glasses to the counter before turning and leaning against it, studying me with narrowed eyes. "Your ex did a real number on you, huh?"

I turned from the sink and leaned against the counter beside him. "I find myself thinking back to everything he ever said and did, trying to figure out what was the truth and what was a big fat lie."

"Doesn't sound like it's doing you any good."

"You're probably right."

"I *am* right," he assured me, his serious tone leaving no room for doubt.

"And what's worse is we're not even divorced yet," I explained. "It takes a while for all the logistics to be worked out."

"That sucks."

"Yep. CJ and I are just biding our time in this house until I can sell it and move somewhere I'll be able to afford on my own." I shrugged. "The one good thing about Charles cheating is he still pays the mortgage. Guilt I assume."

Trace's lips twisted. "CJ's never once mentioned him."

"His dad?"

Trace nodded.

"That's what happens when you move an hour away from your son and barely call him or come by to take him out."

"Someday he'll realize he missed out."

I stepped away from the counter and rolled my eyes. "Would you look at me? I shouldn't be unloading on you like this. I'm sorry."

"You can unload on me anytime you want."

I laughed. "Oh, yeah. That's what all college guys say. Right before they hand you another red cup and lead you somewhere quiet to talk."

He grinned and his damn dimples dug in. "Well, for what it's worth, I'm serious."

I cocked my head. "When I was in college, my biggest problem was deciding which frat party to go to on Saturday night. I assume your problems are pretty similar."

He shook his head. "Football's a huge stressor for me. If I have any chance of going pro, there's no room for failure. I need to stay in shape, know the plays, and work my ass off. And while I may frequent the occasional party, I need to keep my eye on the prize."

"Which is?"

"Winning." His blue eyes moved over my face. "At all costs."

A shiver raced up my spine. "Why do I get the feeling you're not just talking about football?"

His lips twitched. "I like being good at everything I do."

Gah. Why was everything out of his mouth so damn sexy? My mind instantly flashed to dirty places.

I was going to hell. I was going straight. To. Hell.

Trace pushed off the counter. I tipped my head back to look at him as he stood in front of me. "Thanks for lunch."

"Anytime."

He stared down at me for a moment longer, then moved toward the front door and called upstairs. "See you tomorrow, CJ."

"Bye, Trace. Thanks for playing with me," CJ called.
Trace glanced to me. "You raised a hell of a kid."
"Yeah. I did, didn't I?"
His soft laughter followed him out the front door.

CHAPTER FOUR

Marin

Basketball at Trace's house became one of CJ's favorite activities. I felt bad, given football was Trace's sport, but he didn't say a word, doing whatever CJ wanted.

I finished making lunch and walked down to join them. When I neared Trace's house, CJ shot baskets alone. An unfamiliar car sat idling at the end of the driveway while Trace leaned in the passenger window talking to the driver. I wondered how long CJ had been playing alone.

"Hey, buddy," I called to CJ as I walked over.

Trace yanked his head from the window and stood up quickly, stepping back from the car.

CJ's smile eased my fears and he bounced me the ball. "You shoot it, Mom."

I caught it before my eyes wandered to the car. The slightest tinge of jealousy formed in my stomach when I spotted the pretty brunette behind the steering wheel. I turned away from whatever I'd interrupted and shot the ball from where I stood. The damn thing bounced off the rim.

Great one, Marin.

I had no reason to be jealous—or angry for that matter. Trace didn't ask to be a stand-in for CJ's father. I'd cornered him. Put him on the spot. He had a life, and I was in no position to impede on that. I hadn't thought it through. I'd asked on a whim, and now I'd given him a role he never asked for. A role that would end when he returned to school, leaving CJ in the dust. I hadn't considered there was an expiration date to this deal. I'd never considered CJ would become so attached.

I forced a smile as I watched CJ run after my rebound. The smile slipped off my face at the sight of Janine Forester standing in the front window, her eyes narrowed on mine.

"See you later, Mel," Trace said, snatching my attention from his mother just as his friend's car pulled away.

"She didn't have to leave," I said, giving indifference my best attempt.

CJ passed Trace the ball. He caught it and shrugged. "She just wanted to say hey." He shot from quite a distance away and sank it effortlessly.

I watched CJ run to retrieve it, glancing to the window where Janine no longer peered out. I stood there in the driveway, unsure what to say. I suddenly felt like an intruder at Trace's house. "Come on, buddy," I said to CJ. "Time to head home. Lunch awaits."

"I'm not invited?" Trace asked.

My eyes cut to his. "I thought you had work."

He shook his head. "Not tonight."

* * *

Lights from the television flashed over CJ's sleeping body on the rug in my dim living room. I glanced to Trace stretched out on the sofa watching the end of the movie CJ insisted he watch with us after lunch. To an outsider, the scene in my living room would've looked so normal. But for me, I needed to remind myself this wasn't my family.

Once the credits rolled, Trace sat up and looked to me on the love seat. "That knocked him out," he whispered.

"*You* knocked him out," I said just as softly. "He's never had so much exercise in his life."

He laughed. "Hey. A deal's a deal."

"Well, thanks. It means so much to him."

"Just him?"

I cocked my head. "I figured that went without saying."

"It's always nice to hear how amazing I am."

I laughed. "And you're humble."

His shoulders shook with laughter. "That is definitely not something I've ever been called." He pushed himself to his feet, his height imposing as he stood in the middle of my living room. "I've gotta head out."

"Oh, I'm sorry. I didn't mean to keep you here."

"You didn't keep me here, Marin. I only do what I wanna do."

I nodded, standing and walking him around a sleeping CJ to the door. "So, where're you headed?"

He hesitated for a second before he pulled open my front door, the early evening air a stark contrast to the central air in my house. "I've got a date."

An unexpected bout of disappointment washed over me. "With the girl in the car?" I asked, trying to sound unfazed, though the lack of control I had over my emotions these days was becoming unsettling.

He stepped outside, turning back to face me. "Yeah."

I exhaled an envious breath. It had been so long since I'd been on a date. Dinners with Charles had always been with either CJ or with clients. Never the two of us alone laughing and having a good time. "I'm sorry." I shook my head, suddenly aware that I'd been prying. "It's none of my business."

"Sure it is. You should know who I hang out with in case I bring her around CJ."

The whole idea of there being someone he'd want to bring around CJ suddenly sucked. "You two go to school together?"

He shook his head. "Mel couldn't get into college if her daddy was the dean."

I laughed as I grabbed the door handle. "Oh, so you're into the ditzy ones."

The sound of his laughter filled me with an unfamiliar feeling. A terrifying one.

"See," I teased. "I've got you all figured out."

"You think you do."

"I've got my psych degree, you know?"

He tucked his lips, suppressing a smile. "Should that scare me?"

"I have a feeling nothing scares you."

He laughed again and time seemed to stall as his eyes moved over my features.

"What?" I asked, wondering if he was taking in the lines around my eyes that girls his age didn't have yet.

He shook his head. "Nothing."

I glanced at the clock on the TV. "You should probably get going. Don't want you to be late for your date."

He made his way down the front steps, but twisted back to face me. "You busy tomorrow?"

I looked at him curiously. "Busy?"

"Yeah. I wanna take you somewhere."

I swallowed hard.

"I've got something I wanna show you and CJ," he explained.

Of course he meant the two of us. Why would he have just meant me? "Where?"

"Another question? Seriously? Do you have a better offer?"

I tilted my head, laying on the sass. "You haven't told me what you're offering."

"Time with me. Is there anything better?"

My lips twisted as I debated my response. "Not in CJ's book."

"In yours?"

I stared back at him, noncommittal. There wasn't a chance in hell I was touching that one.

"Fine," he relented. "I'll pick you guys up at noon." He turned to walk away, calling over his shoulder. "Oh, and dress comfortably."

As the darkness swallowed him whole, I closed the door and leaned my back against it. What the hell had I just agreed to?

CHAPTER FIVE

Marin

CJ flew out the front door, greeting Trace in the driveway as soon as he stepped out of his black truck. I locked the front door, turning just in time to see Trace help CJ climb in the small backseat, wrapping the seatbelt around him.

"Wait." I motioned toward my car beside his. "I need to grab his booster seat."

"He's all set," Trace said as he shut the back door and rounded the truck to my side, pulling open the front passenger door. "I picked one up."

My mouth parted as I walked toward him. "You bought a booster seat?"

He laughed. "Don't look so surprised. It was like thirty bucks. And I plan on taking him places if that's okay with you."

I shook my head, unable to fully process what he'd done and why he'd done it.

"I've heard puppies, wedding rings, and babies are a major turn-on for women, but you had to see the looks I got carrying the booster seat through the store."

I smiled, grabbing the handrail and pulling myself up into the passenger seat imagining what he must've looked like walking through that store. "You probably should've tried that one sooner."

Trace laughed as he closed my door. Once he sat beside me on the bench seat, he turned to look at me, giving me a once over that sent goosebumps scattering over my skin. His eyes zoned in on my legs. The cutoffs I'd chosen didn't seem so short until they rode up in the seat beside him.

"Where're we going?" CJ asked.

Trace's eyes jumped away, meeting CJ's in the rearview mirror as his truck roared to life. "It's a surprise."

An hour into our trip, CJ had fallen asleep in the backseat. All the exercise he'd been getting with Trace had obviously wiped him out.

"If you're hungry, I packed a lunch," Trace said.

I looked over at him curiously. "You're taking us on a picnic?"

He smiled. "Not exactly, but it's a bit of a ride, so..."

"So you thought you'd pack us a lunch?" I said, stunned anyone other than a mother would've thought ahead like that.

"Don't be too impressed," he laughed. "I just made sandwiches."

I held up my palms. "Hey, I'm not complaining. If I didn't have to make them, it works for me."

He smiled as I turned to my window and gazed out.

"I know where you're taking us," I said, glancing back at him a little while later.

Trace's eyes cut to mine. "Oh, yeah?"

I nodded. "You're taking us to your school."

"How'd you know?"

"It's where I went. I know the way."

"I didn't know that."

I nodded. "Though, I wasn't a nineteen-year-old senior."

His eyes jumped between me and the road. "How do you know how old I am?"

My face fell, my mind searching for a reply that wouldn't make me sound like a crazy person. "Oh, you were like eleven or twelve when I moved in, weren't you? I kind of remember that."

His eyes narrowed, like he didn't completely buy my response. "Yeah."

"But aren't seniors twenty-one?"

"Yeah. But I skipped third grade."

My head retracted. "No way."

He nodded. "Yep. And my birthday's November third, so I'll technically be a twenty-year-old senior instead of the normal twenty-one or twenty-two."

"How's that been?"

"Hasn't hurt me so far."

I shook my head. He could turn any innocent comment into something more.

"You go to any games while you were in school?" he asked, changing the subject from his age.

"Obviously."

He laughed. "Yeah, well, they didn't have a receiver like me."

I shrugged. "I haven't seen you play."

"That sounds like a challenge."

"Nope. Just the truth."

"Well, I assure you, you've never seen a receiver as good as me. I'll get you tickets. Bring CJ."

I nodded. "He'd like that."

"Would you?"

"That remains to be seen."

He snickered.

Our banter came so naturally. And the more time I spent with Trace, the more comfortable I felt with him. I needed a cold-shower-reminder we were just friends. "How'd your date go?"

He shrugged. "As expected."

"What's that mean?"

"She was all over me within the first fifteen minutes, drunk within the first thirty."

"You don't enjoy that?"

"If all I wanted was sex, I know where to look. I'm not an asshole. Conversations are good, too."

I glanced over my shoulder to be sure CJ was still asleep. He was. "Are you gonna see her again?"

He laughed. "Who knows." His eyes cut to mine. "A guy gets lonely when he's home from school."

An unexpected ache crept between my legs. I needed a subject change like yesterday. "So...is professional football the end goal for you or are you majoring in something you're really interested in?"

He smirked. "You mean does the dumb jock have a backup plan?"

My eyes widened. "I didn't say that."

His attention continued alternating between the road and me. "But you were thinking it."

I shook my head. "Not at all. You're a really smart guy."

He laughed. "I was only playing. I'm actually majoring in sports medicine. If I don't make it to the pros—" He pinned me with his eyes. "By some crazy turn of events..."

I laughed.

"I'll go to grad school to major in physical therapy or sports training."

I smiled, once again surprised by this guy who was so much more than meets the eye. He had lofty expectations yet tempered them with realistic goals. He thought ahead. Thought about what happened if he didn't reach his goal. If he failed.

"What about you?" he asked.

"What about me?" It was strange to have someone interested in what I had to say. Charles tended to speak *at* me, not *to* me.

"You said you had a psych degree?"

"Yeah, a Bachelor's. I was in grad school for clinical psychology."

"Was?"

My eyes shifted out the window at the trees speckling the side of the highway, embarrassed to have to admit the reason aloud. "Charles asked me to stop taking classes." *Hind-freaking-sight.*

"So, was becoming a clinical psychologist your end goal?"

I looked to him, appreciating him not telling me how stupid I'd been for listening to Charles. "Yep. But now that I have CJ, I wonder if child psychology or family counseling would have been more fulfilling."

"It's not too late to find out."

"Yeah. I've been thinking a lot about it lately."

"I think you'd be great working with kids," Trace said.

I glanced to him with a grin. "Says the child whisperer. *You'd* be great with kids. You're already great with one kid in particular."

Trace peeked at CJ in the rearview mirror still sound asleep. "Just so we're clear—" He met me with his expressive eyes. "I'm great at *everything* I do."

A shiver skimmed down my spine. He was clearly the king of one-liners—ones that were meant to make girls stupid. I wondered if he was just a tease or a guy who actually delivered. What was I saying? Of course he delivered.

Before long, Trace pulled onto campus. As my eyes moved from left to right, memories flooded me at every turn. The sidewalks. The buildings. The dorms. So many wonderful recollections surrounded me as we moved through campus. Recollections I'd kept locked away. Much like the magic of a beloved song, I was instantly transported to that time and place. Those friends. Those feelings. Those emotions. I'd been so carefree back then. So happy.

Trace pulled into the empty stadium parking lot, parking in front of the entrance. "Wait here," he said as he jumped out, closing the door softly so not to startle CJ, still asleep in the backseat.

He jogged to the main door and pounded on it twice. He buried his hands in the pockets of his cargo shorts and waited. He was so incredibly good looking. I couldn't imagine being able to resist him in college. He was completely my type, and I would've fallen hard for his outgoing and confident personality. There was something to be said for a guy who was so comfortable in his own skin.

How had I forgotten that? Better yet, how had I ended up with Charles?

I guess him being older and already an established lawyer was appealing when I was twenty-one. But I'd forgotten I was a sucker for a great personality. A sense of humor. A good body. Someone I could trust. I'd totally missed the mark with Charles.

The stadium door opened and Trace stepped back, talking to the older man who greeted him. The way the man threw back his head in laughter proved Trace could charm anyone. After a quick conversation, Trace turned and waved us over.

I hopped out of the truck and made my way to CJ's door, opening it. "Come on," I whispered to CJ. "Time to get out."

CJ's eyes opened slowly as he looked around the inside of the truck, trying to get his bearings. His eyes ventured out the window, widening when he saw the massive stadium in front of us.

"Trace took us to his school," I explained as I unbuckled him. "He wants to show us around."

"Awe-some," CJ said as I helped him out of the truck.

With our fingers linked, we walked over to where Trace waited in the doorway.

"Follow me." Trace smiled, proudly leading us through the entrance hall. Vibrant murals of football players filled the lobby walls. Trace looked to CJ and pointed at one of them. "Someday, that'll be me up there."

"*Really?*" CJ said, awed by just about anything Trace said.

We followed Trace down a restricted hallway and into the carpeted locker room. It was meticulously clean and a whole lot nicer than I ever expected for college football players.

CJ's wide eyes took it all in. I loved seeing things through his eyes and this had to be incredibly cool to him.

Trace pointed out his locker and grabbed the stool stored inside, explaining that it sat in front of his locker on game days. He let CJ sit on it, taking a couple pictures of him and sending them to my phone.

From there, he brought us through a tunnel that led down to the football field. We stepped out onto the lush green grass. It was impossible not to take in the grandeur surrounding us. The massive red and white tiers enveloped the field, towering like skyscrapers. I'd been in the seats before, but I'd never seen the stadium from this vantage point. It was breathtaking. I could only imagine how it felt for Trace and his teammates as they ran out to the roar of over one hundred thousand fans on game day.

Trace took off jogging down the field toward the end zone, calling CJ to follow. CJ ran after him, his small legs fighting to catch up as the two of them circled the empty field.

I moved to the nearby bench on the sideline and sat, watching them tackle one another and fall onto their backs in fits of laughter.

"He's good with kids."

My head whipped around. The old man who'd let Trace into the stadium stood with his eyes on Trace and CJ. It was then I noticed the security shield on his red shirt. "Yeah. He's great."

"He's also a hell of a receiver."

"I've never seen him play," I admitted.

The man dropped down beside me on the bench. "Well, I've been here for too many years to count. And I can say, without a shadow of a doubt, that he's one of

the best to come through this program. He's going to
the pros. He's got everything teams need.
Determination. Height. Speed. And he's good with his
hands." He bumped me with his shoulder. "But I don't
have to tell you that now, do I?" He laughed a deep
husky laugh.

"Oh, no. We're just friends," I said. "He spends time
with my son."

His eyes narrowed. "So you and he—"

I shook my head.

"Could've fooled me."

"Why's that?"

He shrugged. "A guy doesn't go out of his way to
bring a girl and her boy here just because they're
friends."

My eyes drifted back out to the field watching them
play like they'd known each other forever. Trace was an
unbelievable guy. And CJ and I were very lucky to be
on the receiving end of his kindness.

The man stuck out his hand. "I'm Arnie."

I shook it. "Marin."

"Hey, Mom. Look at me," CJ shouted, pretending to
kick an imaginary ball through the goal post.

"Nice kick," I called.

"Let me go grab them a ball," Arnie said, pushing
himself to his feet and disappearing through the tunnel.

Trace rounded CJ from behind and tackled him onto
the grass. CJ's laughter filled the empty stadium and
shot right to the cracks in my heart, filling them with
the happiness that should've always been there. I closed
my eyes for a long moment and pulled in a deep
cleansing breath. The days following Charles' infidelity
had been torture. I needed to wear a brave face for CJ,

who was unable to understand why his daddy wasn't coming home. I never thought I'd see him smile, laugh, or have fun again. But he was. And I had Trace to thank for much of that.

"Hey, Forester," Arnie called.

My eyes snapped open. Trace stood with his palms up as Arnie passed him the ball. It fell short, but Trace made quick work of reaching down and scooping it up. "Nice pass, Arnie."

"Ah, getting old stinks."

"Nah, you've still got it," Trace assured him with an easy smile.

Arnie looked to me. "He's one of the good ones."

"Hey, Marin," Trace called. "Get out here and show us what you've got."

"Uh—"

"Don't leave a man waiting," Arnie urged. "Take it from me. Enjoy life while you're still young."

Arnie had no idea how right he was. I may have screwed up by marrying Charles, but I *was* still young and I wouldn't let a screw up dictate how I lived the rest of my life. If I wanted to be miserable, that was my choice. If I wanted to be happy…well, it seemed like a no brainer.

I jumped to my feet. CJ danced around, eager for me to play. Trace passed me the ball. Of course I fumbled it in my hands before holding onto it. I looked to CJ who held up his hands and I tossed him the ball.

"Nice spiral," Trace said.

"I've got mad skills," I said, using Trace's words as I dashed toward CJ. He yelped, before twisting away from me and taking off running.

"Mad skills?" Trace's laughter echoed off the seats as I chased CJ around. "That's hilarious."

I glanced over my shoulder at Trace standing there looking right at home in the massive stadium. "Are you making fun of me?"

He shook his head. "I wouldn't dare."

I snatched the ball from CJ's hands, leaving him stunned as I took off running. He sprinted after me. So did Trace. Trace was faster and he nearly reached me as I shrieked. "Don't!"

"Try and stop me," Trace called as he closed the distance between us.

CJ jumped around with his hands waving over his head. "Pass it here."

I passed it to him just as Trace wrapped his arms around my waist and lifted me off the ground. "Put me down," I begged through laughter.

"Nope. Having way too much fun."

I conceded, allowing myself to relax in his arms with his hard chest pressed to my back. A shiver surged through me. A delicious, content shiver.

Shit. Shit. Shit.

"Come and get me," CJ called.

Both our heads turned to find him jumping around with the ball between his small hands. Trace lowered me to my feet and we took off running toward him. CJ screeched, before turning and bolting in the opposite direction. We trailed him easily. Trace let me grab him first and lift him off his feet. Then Trace grabbed both of us, tackling us gently to the grass. Our laughter filled the stadium, and the happiness I saw in CJ's beautiful green eyes pricked my own eyes with tears. I looked up to find Trace gazing down at me, his blue eyes holding something I couldn't quite read, but I could say with much certainty that it scared the hell out of me.

I was in big freaking trouble.

CHAPTER SIX

Marin

I slipped on my nude heels as I hobbled my way down the stairs Friday night. My parents sat on the sofa on both sides of CJ pretending to be interested in whatever he was showing them on his tablet.

"You look gorgeous," my dad said, his eyes taking in the navy off-the-shoulder dress I'd pulled from the back of my closet.

I laughed, stopping at the bottom of the stairs and fixing my dress into place. "You're my dad. You have to say that."

"Well, I think you look beautiful, too," my mom added.

"Me too," CJ said without bothering to look up.

"Thanks." I glanced between my parents. "I shouldn't be late."

"Stay out as late as you want. We're taking him back to our house," my mom said.

"Woo hoo!" CJ shouted, dropping his tablet and jumping up to dance around the living room like a little nut. "Can I stay all weekend?"

"We'll see," I said, making sure my parents knew they didn't have to give in to his every wish.

"Just keep your head up," my mom reminded me.

I nodded as I grabbed my sparkly clutch from the table and stopped at the front door. "Well, wish me luck."

* * *

I walked into the ballroom at the Silver Lake Country Club, somehow mixing up the times and missing the ceremony all together. I sent up a silent prayer that the bride and groom put me with other singles, and not a bunch of happy couples. I eyed the numbers beneath the tall floral centerpieces draping down to the tables, locating table twenty in the back corner of the room. Since I was only Felecia and Seamus' neighbor, I didn't expect to be in the front of the room.

I approached the already filled table searching for the only empty chair, making a beeline straight for it. I lifted my gaze to greet my tablemates, surprised to find all my neighbors, including Trace and the brunette from the car—Mel—staring at me. My heart tripped over itself. "Hi."

"Hey," Trace said, clearly surprised to see me as he jumped to his feet and pulled out the empty chair beside him. The navy tie over his white button down brought out the intensity in his eyes as they assessed me up and down.

"Thanks." I slipped into the chair, wishing goosebumps hadn't coasted up my bare arms as I brushed by him. Once I settled into my seat, I glanced at everyone, including Trace's parents. "How's everyone doing?"

They all smiled and greeted me warmly, though I wondered what they were really thinking of me being there alone.

"No date tonight, Marin?" Trace's mom called across the table, answering my question for me.

I swallowed down the sudden lump lodged in my throat and maintained my composure. I wasn't about to allow Janine Forester to make me feel any more uncomfortable than I already did. I'd known her long enough to know it was her MO. Make others feel inferior and then she maintained the upper hand in every situation. Thankfully, her son was *nothing* like her. "Nope. Just me."

She gave me the once over. "It's a shame to waste such a pretty dress on no one special."

"Mom," Trace hissed at the same time his father hissed, "Janine."

"It's okay," I whispered.

"No, it's not," Trace muttered under his breath.

I knew enough to keep my distance from Trace, especially under his mother's watchful eye, not to mention his date sitting there anticipating all his attention. So I looked to Steve, my neighbor who'd lost his wife last year, seated on my other side. "How are you doing, Steve?"

Steve shrugged, his outdated brown suit wrinkled from lack of use. "Hanging in there."

A waiter approached our table carrying a tray of champagne. "I'll have one." I didn't wait for him to place it down, just took it from his hand and finished it off in one long gulp. As he rounded the table after serving the others, I handed him my empty glass and grabbed another. He chuckled under his breath. He had no idea.

Trace bumped me softly with his shoulder. I swiveled to face him. "This is Mel," he said before looking to his date. "Mel, Marin."

"Hi," I said, wondering if she remembered me from Trace's house. *And* if her short dress was an indication of the type of girl Trace went for.

"How's your son, Marin?" Janine asked, obviously working an angle. She'd seen CJ and me at her house. Didn't she know how much time Trace spent with us? "Great."

She leaned toward Mel who sat beside her and whispered loud enough for me to hear. "Her husband left her and their young boy."

"Mom," Trace growled. "That's enough."

Anger bubbled inside me as heat pulsed in my cheeks. There wasn't a chance in hell I planned to hold my tongue, especially with the champagne already beginning to work its magic. "Actually," I said, my eyes moving to Trace's date. "I kicked his sorry ass out."

Trace choked.

"Yeah," I continued, apparently on a roll. "Couldn't keep it in his pants." I looked to Janine. "Thanks for bringing it up, though. I wasn't sure if everyone knew the truth. Wouldn't want the wrong gossip being spread around." I tilted my head condescendingly. "You know what I mean?"

I chewed down my prime rib a little while later, the meat as hard to stomach as the tension at the table. The cake cutting couldn't come quickly enough. Between the glares from Janine, the laughter from Mel because of something Trace whispered in her ear, and Steve telling me stories about his late wife, this night needed to be over.

Our table eventually cleared out as my table mates took to the dance floor. Felecia, the bride, dragged me out there for her favorite girl anthem, but I returned to the table once the DJ informed us he'd be rolling out the slow jams.

Steve had disappeared, so I sat alone wondering if I could slip out unnoticed. The majority of the couples were on the dance floor, including Trace and Mel, who gazed up at him, undoubtedly smitten by his looks and charm. I missed that feeling. That utter bliss accompanying a new relationship. That knowledge that someone wanted you as much as you wanted them. I wondered what they'd do after the wedding. Would he take her right home? Or would he take her somewhere private?

The song ended and another slow one began. I averted my gaze from the dance floor and eyed the exit. Steve stood by it. I could speak to him, and then sneak out. Yep. That's what I'd do. I grabbed my clutch and stood.

Shit.

I grasped the back of the chair, steadying myself on my heels. Apparently, the liquor had caught up with me. Great. Now I either needed to sober up or call an Uber. Could the night get any worse?

A large hand landed on my bare arm sending chills rushing over my skin. My head twisted.

Trace stood there in his loosened tie. "Dance with me."

My eyes shot around to all the couples swaying to the song drifting through the speakers. "Where's your date?"

"Bathroom."

I glanced back to him. "I don't think we should."

His face grew incredulous. "Why not?"

"Your mother. She'll probably get on the microphone and tell the entire room my business."

His hand slipped down my arm until his fingers linked with mine. I wished my hand didn't feel so small in his. It only made me see him as the man I was beginning to wish he was. He tugged me gently onto the dance floor, stopping us in the corner, far from prying eyes.

When he turned to face me, I considered where to place my hands. I didn't want to do anything that would look inappropriate and add more fuel to Janine's fire.

"Put your arms around my neck."

"I know where they go," I mumbled, more embarrassed than anything else. I lifted my hands and rested them on his shoulders, one hand still grasping my clutch. Trace's fresh aloe scent overwhelmed my senses as he slipped his hands around my back. They were firm and strong and pulled me against his solid chest. Having his arms around me in the stadium had been playful. This was intimate.

Before I knew it, we were swaying in time to the music. His muscular grip reminded me what it was like to be in the arms of someone strong. Someone who wanted to be there with me. I wondered if he could feel my racing heart. I tipped my head to look up at him. He was already staring down at me. The look in his eyes was not the look he'd given Mel while they danced. This one held hunger. My body hummed like a crazy live wire. It was wrong. It was so incredibly wrong to be feeling this way. "Your date's nice," I said, trying to alleviate the awkwardness of being in his arms in a room full of people.

"She just offered to fuck me in the bathroom."

I blinked hard, taken aback by his response. "Oh."

He laughed. "You've gotta see the look on your face right now."

I shook off my surprise. "Does that sort of thing happen to you often?"

He shrugged. And everything about the way his shoulders lifted beneath my hands told me it did.

My eyes flashed over Trace's shoulder. Janine stared at us across the dance floor. Her glaring eyes screamed one thing. Me dancing with her son was not okay. My attention glided back to Trace and his piercing blue eyes. "So, you didn't want to take her up on her offer?"

His laughter hit me deep, probably because his chest rumbled against mine. "The idea of my dad walking in and finding us going at it in the bathroom wasn't on my list of things to do tonight."

"So later?" I could *not* believe I asked that.

"Later?" He pulled back slightly, his eyes narrowed.

"Yeah. You'll wait until later."

He said nothing, just stared at me. I had no idea what he searched for as his eyes riveted between mine. All I knew was his arms tightening around me felt way too right. "Come by the bar tomorrow."

"What?"

"I want you to come by the bar."

"CJ's at my mom and dad's house."

"I didn't say CJ. I said you."

Tingles shot between my thighs. "Oh."

"*Oh*, you'll come?" He flashed his crooked smile, the one that said he knew something I didn't. "Or *oh*, you'll wuss out?"

The song ended and I abruptly stepped back and out of his arms, not wanting to linger too long or give myself a chance to say or do something I would've regretted with a clear head in the morning. "Thanks for the dance. Now I don't feel like a complete loser coming to a wedding alone." I turned to walk away.

Trace grabbed my arm and pulled me back to face him. "So?" His face inched closer to mine. "Should I expect you?"

My eyes zoned in on his lips. What would they feel like? What would they taste like? *Shit. Shit. Shit.* "I don't think so."

"Wuss."

My eyes lifted to his. "Maybe."

"Maybe you'll show or maybe you're a wuss?" he asked.

"I guess you'll just have to wait and find out." I spun on my heels, knowing they accented my killer quads, and walked off the dance floor. Instead of leaving, I turned into the ladies' room and stood in the back of the short line, taking a much-needed deep breath.

What was it about Trace that set me off balance?

And why did he have to be so young?

"I wish he looked at me the way he looks at you."

My eyes shot around, searching for the familiar voice.

Mel walked out of a stall and up to the sink. Her eyes met mine in the mirror.

"Excuse me?"

"Forester. The way he looks at you. Don't tell me you can't see it?"

"You must be mistaken."

She shook her head. "Nope. He gave you the look. And if I'm being honest, he's been giving you the same look all night."

"What look?"

She rubbed her hands together under the faucet. "The one that says I've got plans for you and me."

I hesitated. "You got that from a look?"

She switched off the faucet and grabbed a paper towel. "I got that from knowing how he works. And Forester hasn't had to work for it since he hit puberty."

She spun to face me while drying her hands. "A word to the wise. If you want a piece, don't play so hard to get. He'll get bored and move on. And from what I've heard, there's one hell of a line on campus."

"Why are you telling me this?"

She tossed her paper towel into the garbage and turned back to me. "If I'm not getting any action, someone should be."

With that she disappeared out of the ladies' room, leaving me with her words and the realization that I had absolutely no idea what I was doing when it came to Trace Forester.

CHAPTER SEVEN

Trace

My shift had been a slow one for a Saturday night. Football fans had planted their asses at the beach-side bar hoping to catch my eye. That's why Lou hired me to bartend even though I was underage. I drew a crowd. The guys wanted to talk ball. The girls…well, they wanted to go home with me. Little did they know I lived at home with my parents for the summer.

I pulled my phone from my pocket, checking it for the umpteenth time. Marin hadn't called. I couldn't believe she blew me off. I wasn't used to girls running from me. She was obviously scared of me. Scared of what I made her feel. I could tell by the way she tried not to relax in my arms when we danced last night. By the way her heart raced against mine as I pulled her closer. By the way she disappeared from the wedding right after our dance. She didn't trust herself with me.

I was certainly a force to be reckoned with. I guess I didn't blame her. I was only home for another month with practice starting up the first week of August.

I wiped down the top of the bar, knowing I had about a half an hour before my dinner break.

"I'll have a Corona with a lime."

A smile spread across my face before my eyes even had a chance to lift to see her. Marin sat on the corner stool to my left, wearing a white top with a sparkly blue necklace that matched her eyes. She looked like any other college girl spending the night at a beach bar.

"Well, hello," I said.

She smiled coyly.

I loved that she showed up. And I wanted to know so damn bad why she had. Was it because I asked her to or because she wanted to see me? "What brings you to these parts?"

"It's been awhile since I've been here. Thought I'd check it out."

"That the only reason?" I reached into the cooler and grabbed her beer, snapping off the top with an opener under the bar.

"Heard the service was okay."

I lifted a brow as I pinched a lime into the bottle. "Just okay?"

She shrugged.

I handed her the bottle, purposely grazing my fingertips over hers. It was probably the reason she chugged half the beer before placing it down on the bar. I glanced around. The eyes of most of the guys were on her. Who could blame them? Her wavy blond hair hung over her shoulders. And the highlights framing her face made her look like she spent hours on the beach every day. "Glad you made it."

"Wouldn't want anyone thinking I was a wuss." She smiled as she lifted the bottle to her lips.

I loved the way she came across so confident and so in charge even though I knew how vulnerable she was. It intrigued me. Made me want her to step out of her comfort zone, especially when it came to me.

Once my dinner break came, I motioned Marin to follow me toward the beach. She did, slipping off her sandals before stepping onto the sand. The sun sat low on the horizon as we walked toward one of the vacant lifeguard chairs. "You expect me to climb?" she asked, amused by the notion.

"I could always toss you over my shoulder and carry you."

She laughed as she climbed the plank steps and planted her cute ass on the seat. Too bad she'd worn skinny jeans and not those hot as hell cutoffs she'd worn the day we drove to campus. Her ass looked amazing.

Once I reached the top, I sat beside her, purposely pressing my arm and leg against hers, giving her no space of her own. Her faint lavender scent mixed with the brine of the beach.

"Do you take a lot of girls up here?" she asked over the rolling of the waves.

"A lot of girls?"

"Yeah. Mel told me you just snap your fingers and you have your pick."

I laughed a humorless laugh. I was going to kill Mel. "That's not exactly how it works. I actually clap my hands."

Marin laughed, and the raspy sound did weird things to me. It wasn't contrived. It was authentic and all woman.

"So now that we've established I'm funny, thanks for coming."

She shrugged, her eyes moving toward the ocean.

"No, I'm serious. I totally thought you'd be a no show."

"Always keep them guessing," she mused. "That's the mistake I made with—"

"The douchebag," I interrupted. "From here on out we refer to him as the douchebag, if we have to refer to him at all."

She chuckled.

The sun lowered, its edges a hazy fiery vision slowly disappearing beneath the ocean line. I slipped my arm around the back of the chair, gauging Marin's reaction. I would've liked for her to rest her head against my shoulder. But she stayed put, watching the sun set in her own space.

"It's so beautiful," she said, awed by the sight I got to witness every time I worked.

"*You're* so beautiful."

Her body tensed, though her attention stayed on the sunset. "Stop it."

"Stop what?"

"Trying to embarrass me."

"I'm just telling it like it is. And you're fucking beautiful."

She threw back her head and the sound of her laughter carried over the waves.

"What's so funny?" I asked.

Her slender shoulders shook as her laughter slowly subsided. "You. The way you always just say what you're thinking."

"Why wouldn't I?"

She shrugged. "I don't know. I guess I'm just jealous of your boldness."

"You could be bold."

"Yeah, I could be a lot of things. If only I could speak to my younger self."

"What would you say?"

A dry laugh escaped her as the wind gently tousled her hair around her face. "What *wouldn't* I say?"

I reached up and tucked a strand behind her ear. "Come on. Tell me."

"Okay…" Her eyes drifted away as she considered it. "Now, I had quite a bit of fun, especially in college, but I'd still tell myself to have more fun. To live it up."

"More fun is good," I agreed.

"I wouldn't be so concerned with what I ate. I'd pig out more knowing I've got a killer metabolism."

I laughed.

"And I definitely wouldn't have been in such a rush to settle down after graduation."

"So, you'd sleep around?"

She actually thought about my question for a long time. "I'd weigh my options. I was so set on getting into a relationship. Getting a guy to want to settle down with me and love me. I never considered I'd choose the wrong guy."

"There's nothing wrong with wanting a relationship...I guess."

"See." She bumped her shoulder into my arm. "What guy wants a girl who's all about commitment?"

"I'm not against commitment," I countered. "I just need to find the right girl. And not many have the ability to tame this." I glanced down at myself, trying to get her to laugh.

She did, and I was starting to like her laugh way more than I probably should. "Is that what the line you've got forming on campus is all about? Finding the one who can tame you?"

I was *seriously* going to kill Mel. "I call it having fun and sowing my wild oats."

"Oats, huh?"

I laughed. "Isn't that what they say?"

"I don't know who says it. But yeah."

We watched the last of the sun creep down until darkness surrounded us. I liked being around Marin. And the more time I spent with her, the more I wanted to be around her.

Marin

"Sorry about my mom." Trace said as I stared out at the ocean from atop the lifeguard chair.

"She can't help herself."

"That's no excuse. She needs to stay out of other people's business."

"I guess having a cheat for a husband makes for good gossip." I wasn't sure I'd ever get used to the idea that I'd been cheated on. That I'd become gossip. That I looked like a fool.

"Well it's no one's business. Especially my mom's."

I shrugged again. "I don't care. I'm just glad to be rid of him."

"Damn straight you are."

I laughed, loving how everything was so cut and dry with Trace. "I really wish I could see the world through your eyes."

"My eyes?"

"Yeah. Eyes that haven't been tainted by reality. By embarrassment. By heartbreak."

"Just because I'm younger than you, doesn't mean I haven't been hurt or embarrassed."

I cocked my head. "Says the nineteen-year-old."

"I'm serious. The time the picture of my ass went viral, sure I was proud of the angle, but all the attention I got after was damn embarrassing."

I snorted, which only seemed to egg him on.

"And when Julie Jones broke my heart freshman year in high school, I may have listened to my fair share of sad songs in my dark bedroom."

"I don't believe you."

"I swear."

A comfortable silence filled the space between us. Conversations with Trace were so effortless. They'd never been that way with Charles. He was always preoccupied with his phone or his work. When I spoke, I never even knew if he was listening. Chances were he wasn't.

"CJ's leaving Monday to spend some time with his father," I said, having waited all day to tell Trace the news I'd received earlier.

Trace's head turned quickly. "What?"

"I just found out. He'll be gone for a week. Maybe two."

His features darkened. "Why?"

I shrugged. "I assume Charles is trying to figure out if he has time for a child. My lawyer told me I need to let him go or I risk Charles doing something foolish like fighting for physical custody to spite me."

Trace balked at the ridiculousness. "You know there's no way he has time for a kid."

"That's what I'm hoping. I just fear he's trying to look like father of the year in front of his lawyer friends. How would it look if he said he didn't want custody of his own son?"

Trace shook his head. "He's such an asshole."

"No argument here."

"What am I gonna do without my little buddy?" Trace said.

Tears pooled in my eyes. "Don't get me started. I've been crying all day."

Trace dropped his arm from the back of the chair down around my shoulder and pulled me into his side.

I let him. It didn't feel strange. It felt the way it should feel when someone cared about you. Someone cared about your child. If I was being honest, it was the reason I'd shown up. I needed Trace's strength. I need his perspective. Tears streamed down my cheeks. "I just don't want him to turn CJ against me. He's so conniving. I'm scared I'll get the call that CJ wants to stay with him."

"That'll never happen. CJ adores you."

"God, I'm so pathetic. I'm always unloading on you. You must think I'm so ridiculous."

"Nope. I think you're pretty amazing." Trace pulled back so he could see my face. His eyes were serious as he lifted his thumbs to the tears on my cheeks and wiped them away. "When I stop by to say goodbye, I'm gonna let the douchebag know I'll beat his ass if CJ comes back changed."

I offered a small smile, completely believing Trace would do it. I would've given anything to see Charles' face. He was such a wimp next to Trace. He was the complete opposite. "He's leaving around noon."

"I'm gonna miss him."

"He's gonna miss you, too," I assured him.

"Damn straight he is."

I laughed through my tears.

Trace sat up. "What do you say we take a walk?"

"It's been a long time since anyone's asked me to take a walk."

"Now isn't that a damn shame."

"Does it still mean a walk or is there more to it?"

He smiled as he turned and climbed down the steps. "It can be whatever you want it to be."

Despite the nervous knot swelling in my throat, I climbed down the steps. My feet sank into the sand as I stared out at the long stretch of beach on either side of us. Trace slid his hand into mine, holding it tightly.

I sucked in a breath. It was wrong to hold hands with a teenager. Wrong to want his affection. Wrong to believe his compassion, looks, and body made him a man. I tried unlatching my fingers, but Trace just held on tighter.

"We're all alone on this dark beach. No one's around. Can't a guy just hold a girl's hand?"

I opened my mouth to respond—

"Great," Trace said, tugging me toward the water without giving me a chance to respond.

My bare feet slapped against the wet sand as we walked along the shore. The last time I'd been at the beach was the day after learning the truth about Charles. I sat in the water all day just letting the waves conceal my tears as they knocked me down. CJ found it hysterical while I felt like I'd never be able to stand on my own two feet again.

But I was. I was actually doing it.

"What are you thinking about?" Trace asked.

"Just thinking."

We continued walking in silence.

I looked to Trace. His profile was like an etching against the darkening sky. "You're not gonna pry?"

"Tonight's about moving forward."

"Forward," I mused. "I can do that."

"With me?"

"Ha."

"What's so funny?"

I shook my head, amused, flattered, and scared as hell that he might've been serious. "You're too cute for your own good."

"Cute?" A flicker of amusement lit his eyes. "I haven't been called cute since I was ten. Charming, maybe. Hot, definitely. God? Every damn time."

I laughed as the wind whipped my hair into my face.

"Think about it, Marin."

"Think about what?" I asked, pushing the hair out of my eyes.

"Me."

I rolled my eyes. "You're kinda hard not to."

I expected him to respond with something cocky, but he just stared out at the water. I looked out at it too, wondering what he saw. "You up for a skinny dip?"

I shook my head, amused. "You need to get back to work."

"Don't try to get out of it. You said you would've had more fun if given the chance."

"And skinny dipping is fun?" I challenged.

"With me it is."

I laughed.

"Does that mean you're in?" His brows bounced suggestively.

I glanced down at the dark water washing up on the shore and over our feet. "Maybe I could be persuaded."

"Yeah?"

There was something about being with Trace that made me feel gutsy. Made me throw caution to the wind.

"So, what'll it take?" he asked.

I lifted my chin toward his chest. "Lose the shirt."

His lips slipped into a crooked grin. And without hesitation, he grabbed the shirt at the back of his neck and pulled it off.

Holy hell. My eyes zoned in on the defined surface of his freaking chest. I hadn't seen someone so perfect since I was in college.

"Marin?"

My eyes jumped to his.

He lifted his chin at me. "Lose yours."

Now that I'd thrown down the gauntlet, I wasn't sure I could actually go through with it. I lowered my hands and gripped the hem of my shirt, toying with the cotton fabric.

What was I doing? Had I lost my mind?

I released the material.

The disappointment in Trace's eyes was hard to miss. I felt it too. *Ah, hell.* My fingers lowered slowly to the button on my jeans. Trace's eyes followed. Without talking myself out of it, I slipped the button through the slot and shimmied out of my jeans. My shirt covered enough of my red thong to conceal me and make me less self-conscious—and less like I was making a monumental mistake.

Trace's eyes zoned in on mine, though I could see in the way his features tightened that it took tremendous effort for him not to venture a glance down.

I nodded toward his legs. "Now your shorts."

"Now your shirt," he countered as he slipped off his shorts and stood there in his boxers.

I shook my head. "The shirt stays on tonight."

"So, next time?"

"*If* there's a next time, I'll consider it."

"Oh, there'll be a next time," he assured me, right before his eyes dropped to my legs. His grin turned my insides to mush. Complete and utter mush.

What the *hell* was I doing letting him stand there and gawk at me in my underwear?

I turned and bolted into the water, squealing as the chill of the water stabbed at my skin like hundreds of pointy little knives. Trace's laughter carried from the beach before I lowered myself underwater. When I surfaced, I pushed my hair back from my face. It was the complete opposite of the last time I'd been there. This was refreshing, and liberating, and fun as hell.

"I've gotta say," Trace said as he moved to the edge of the water with a giant grin. "I didn't think you'd do it."

"I'm just full of surprises."

"That you are."

"Aren't you coming in?"

He shook his head.

I threw back my head in laughter. It didn't even bother me that he wasn't joining me *or* that my wet shirt clung to my body. Trace had known what I needed. And he made it happen.

He smiled as he stepped back and scooped up his clothes. "Come on. I gotta get back to work."

I smiled as I watched him pull his shirt over his head.

He ticked his head toward the parking lot. "I've got a towel in my truck."

"You don't think I'm capable of staying in here by myself?"

"Oh, no. You're capable. I just don't feel like worrying about you all alone."

"I'll be okay."

Trace stared across the space between us. "Yep, you will."

And for the first time in a long time, I actually believed I would.

"Now, get outta there," he said. "Before I have to come in and get you myself."

I lifted my brows. "I'm not scared."

He threw back his head and laughed. "You should be."

I shuddered. And as much as I wanted to blame the cold water, I knew the real cause. I made my way out of the water toward Trace who met me with his shorts offered.

"Here. Put these on. There's no way you're getting those jeans on yet."

I grabbed his shorts and pulled them on, holding the waist to keep them up as they were sizes too large.

"Come on," he said, wrapping an arm around me and guiding me toward his truck. Given the cool ocean air biting at my wet skin, the warmth of his body was beyond welcome. Once Trace grabbed the towel from his truck, he wrapped it around me. I made fast work of drying myself up and slipping his now wet shorts down my legs with the towel still around me.

"Sorry."

He laughed as he took them from me, pulling a dry pair from his truck. "I always come prepared."

"I don't doubt it."

He howled with laughter. "I am definitely rubbing off on you."

I shrugged. "Could be worse."

He chuckled as he tugged on his shorts. "Worse, huh?"

"Forester!" a deep voice called. "What the hell are you doing? Your break ended half an hour ago."

Trace grimaced. "Duty calls."

"Thanks for inviting me."

"Thanks for showing up, wuss."

"You can't call me that anymore."

His lips pressed into a tight line. "I guess you're right."

I nodded.

"I'll see you," Trace said, turning and walking back to the bar in no particular rush.

CHAPTER EIGHT

Marin

CJ sat on the edge of his bed jamming stuffed animals into his luggage. I dropped down beside him, handing him the cell phone I'd bought for him.

Surprise filled his eyes. "You're giving me a phone?"

I nodded.

"But I'm only five."

I laughed, loving him more than I ever thought possible. "It's so you can call me whenever you want to."

He stared down at it like he feared it would detonate if he moved.

"It doesn't have apps or anything." I pointed to the screen. "You can just make calls. I already set it. Press this button to call me. And this one to call Grandma and Grandpa."

He glanced up at me with inquisitive eyes. "What about Trace?"

I tilted my head. "Oh, honey. Trace is busy."

"Not too busy for me."

Visions of Trace stripping down on the beach flooded my brain. Saturday night had been so much more than I expected when I decided to show up at the bar. Now I understood CJ's awe of Trace. Trace had this way of making you feel like you were the most important person in the world when he was around. "Okay. But only if you promise not to bother him."

CJ's smile reached all the way up to his innocent little eyes. "Promise."

I took his phone and programmed Trace's number in, wondering where he was. He said he wanted to say goodbye to CJ and he was leaving in a few minutes.

"I think you should marry Trace," CJ said.

My eyes shot up. "What?"

"You smile a lot when he's here."

"I do?"

CJ nodded. "And you laugh too."

"I always smile and laugh."

He shook his head. "Not the way you do when he's around."

I wrapped my arm around his small little shoulders and pulled him into me. "I'm gonna miss you."

"I'm gonna miss you more," he said.

Trace

Already late for the afternoon shift I'd picked up at the bar, I jogged up Marin's front walkway, hoping I hadn't missed CJ. The expensive sedan in the driveway told me I hadn't. I knocked on the front door.

After a minute, it swung open and Marin's ex stood in front of me. His brows knitted together, his eyes assessing me up and down. He clearly didn't remember me. "Can I help you?"

"Are CJ and Marin here?"

His eyes narrowed and his voice deepened, as if to scare me. "Who are you?"

"Trace."

His head shot back, his eyes looking me up and down again, this time more in amazement than anger. "Little Trace? The one who rode his skateboard around here like a wild child? Boy, you grew up."

"It happens."

He crossed his arms and leaned against the doorway as if he planned to stand there and shoot the shit with me. "What brings you over?"

"I heard CJ was leaving. I wanted to say goodbye."

"You know CJ?"

"Marin has me hang out with him. You know—" My eyes took in the cheating asshole with nothing but disdain. I hoped he could see it in my face. Feel it in the coldness I was exuding. "She wants a man around for him."

His face sobered and he stood up taller, puffing out his chest like there was anything under his pressed shirt to actually puff out. "He has a man. I'm his father."

I held up my palms, like his tone intimidated me. "Never said you weren't."

"Well, CJ's busy saying goodbye to his mom. I'll tell him you stopped by." The door slammed in my face before I could tell him I'd wait.

Fucking asshole.

I spun away from the door, never wanting to kick the shit out of someone more than I did him in that moment.

Marin

Walking CJ downstairs was one of the hardest things I ever had to do. Everything in me wanted to hold onto him and never let him go. But Charles was his father. And a boy needed his father. And I needed to be sure I didn't do anything to push Charles to fight for physical custody.

My skin crawled as Charles greeted us with a big smile as we stepped into the living room, like he hadn't single-handedly destroyed our family.

"Were you on the phone?" I asked him.

"No," he said.

"Oh, I thought I heard you talking down here."

He shrugged before looking to CJ. "Ready, buddy?"

CJ glanced to me and I nodded encouragingly, though all I wanted to do was cry and beg Charles not to take him. And where was Trace? Not only had he promised to say goodbye, but he promised to instill a little fear in Charles.

Charles took CJ's luggage from him and walked toward the front door. I prayed Trace would be standing there when he pulled it open. He wasn't.

CJ turned to me as Charles walked outside. I squatted down and he wrapped his arms around me. "Do I have to go?" he whispered.

Tears blurred my vision as I hugged him with everything I had. "Your dad wants to spend time with you. I get to do it every day. He wants to spoil you, too."

CJ giggled. "Okay."

"I love you," I said.

"More than the universe?"

I laughed. "More than anything in this whole wide world and any other world that might exist out there."

"I thought so."

I pulled back to look at him, forcing a smile. "Don't forget to call me whenever you want."

"Okay."

I stood and took his hand, walking him to the door. "I'll see you soon."

He nodded, and with that, he hopped down the front steps and met Charles at the open backseat door, disappearing inside. I watched as Charles buckled him in and then closed the door. Charles turned to me and waved. I didn't wave back. I just glared at him, hoping all the hatred I felt for him was conveyed in my eyes.

* * *

Drinking alone on my sofa was so cliché. But CJ had been gone for eleven hours and fifteen minutes. And already I knew I wasn't going to be able to handle the time apart. What if he came back changed? What if he didn't miss me?

I lifted the beer to my lips and chugged the contents. What would I do with so much time alone? My friends all had families. They had their own lives. Sure, they might be up for shopping from time to time, but I didn't have the money to blow now that I had bills to pay and hadn't found a job yet.

If only I'd finished my Master's degree. If only I hadn't listened to Charles who wanted me home, preferring a wife who cleaned the house and had dinner on the table instead of one who worked long hours, like him. Being naïve and in my early twenties, I went along with his wishes, not realizing I was losing a piece of myself in the process. Now, I had a depleting bank account and a soon-to-be-ex-husband.

I grabbed my phone from the coffee table and scrolled through my contacts, wondering who I could bother. It wasn't even midnight yet. My single friends were probably still up, if not out. After all, the night was still young.

Speaking of young.

My thumbs pounded away at the screen. **Thx for coming to see CJ.** It took everything in me not to add "you big fat jerk."

Trace's text popped up almost immediately. **You're welcome.**

That. Jerk. My thumbs went to work. **He really wanted to see you.**

I really wanted to see him too.

I gasped at his nerve. **Well then, we're in agreement. You suck.**

There was a long pause before those three dots appeared indicating he was typing. **Open your door.**

I sucked in a sharp breath. My eyes shifted to the front door. I didn't hear anything on the other side. And I wasn't foolish enough to actually get up and look.

Pounding on the door froze me to my spot. *Shit.*

I didn't want to see him after he let CJ down.

The pounding continued.

Dammit.

I pushed myself to my feet and unlocked the door, yanking it open. "What?"

Trace stood there like he'd just rolled out of bed. He was barefoot in a white sleeveless T-shirt and basketball shorts that hung low on his hips. "*What?* What the hell was that text about?"

I dug my hands into my hips. "I thought you wanted to say goodbye?"

"I did."

A harsh laugh burned in my throat. "Well, did you have something better to do?"

His face scrunched up. "What are you talking about?"

"It would've taken two minutes to come by."

"I did come by," his voice raised incredulously. "The douchebag wouldn't let me see him."

My eyes rounded. "You came by?" Tremors rocked through my body as his eyes slowly descended over the booty shorts and tank top I wore to bed.

"You texted and thanked me," he said.

"I was being sarcastic."

He peered inside my living room at the empty bottles on the coffee table. His eyes jumped back to mine. "Did you drunk-text me?"

I crossed my arms, suddenly feeling foolish—and in need of something to cover me up.

"You did," he said, his smile growing. "That's fucking hilarious." His brows lifted. "Were you thinking about me?"

"Yeah. And I wanted to clock you for not saying goodbye."

He moved forward. I had no choice but to step back into my house. Once inside and on even ground, he closed the door behind him and stared down at me. "Clock me or fuck me?"

My core quivered at the ease in which the words slipped out of his mouth. At my tipsiness and how damn hot he looked. At the notion that he may have been right. I swallowed hard. "I...uh..." I spun away from him, hurrying toward the kitchen. "You want something to drink?" I stopped short, spinning to face him. "What am I even saying? I can't offer you a drink."

"No, but I can go in your fridge and grab my own."

"I could stop you."

He smirked as he moved toward me, each step closing the distance between us.

My heart thrashed around inside my chest. *Oh God.* I was in no way equipped to make a smart decision. If he tried to kiss me, I just might let him.

He didn't.

Instead, he brushed by me and stepped into the kitchen. "I'd love to see you try."

The breath I hadn't meant to hold whooshed out of me. I walked into the kitchen, unable to stop my eyes from appreciating the way his shirt gripped his back and his shorts hung on those muscular hips. At the way he moved with such grace for a big guy. At the way he always just fit in my space. I didn't stand a freaking chance alone with him. "What'd you do tonight?" I asked, trying to ease the sexual tension radiating off the walls.

He grabbed the refrigerator door handle and looked to me. "I waited for your text."

I tilted my head, calling his bluff. "How'd you know I'd text?"

He smirked. "Because we had fun at the beach. And because you're lonely."

I stood silently, unsure what to say. He was right on both accounts.

"I just never imagined I'd get lucky enough to be your drunk text." He pulled the refrigerator door open and reached inside.

The jingle of bottles sped up my already erratic heartbeat. If I wasn't the voice of reason, things could get real. Fast. "Will I get arrested?"

He laughed. "What do you expect to happen tonight?"

I pinched the bridge of my nose, unable to deal with him and his flirting. "I meant the beer."

He closed the fridge with two beers in his hand. "Well, that's too bad."

I struggled to maintain what little composure I had left. "Let me get a bottle opener." I reached into the nearby utensil drawer. What was I doing? What the *hell* was I doing?

I felt the heat of Trace's body move behind me. I froze, closing my eyes to gather what sanity I still possessed.

"When was the last time he touched you?" Trace's breath fanned over my bare shoulders.

"What?" my voice quivered.

He placed the bottles down on the counter.

Ohmigod.

His hands landed on my shoulders. The warmth emanating from his touch seared my skin as his hands moved slowly down my arms. "You deserve to be touched by a real man."

A delicious shiver rolled through me. *Shiiiit.*

"Growing up, you were in every one of my fantasies, Marin."

Goosebumps scampered over my skin as I swallowed down my nerves.

His hands drifted back up my arms, slowly, possessively. "I haven't been able to stop thinking about you in the water." He stepped into me, shifting his hips so his erection pressed against my ass.

The ache between my legs came hard and fast, nearly bringing me to my knees.

"Did you realize I could see your lacy bra through your wet shirt?"

"No," I whispered because it was all I could muster.

"And that thong. That *fucking* thong," he rasped. "Did you realize how badly you'd be teasing me?"

I squeezed my eyes, my body humming with want and need. I'd never felt so compelled to touch someone before. Someone I shouldn't. The urge prickled my fingers, static electricity pulsing in the tips. I couldn't stop myself. I reached over my shoulder letting my fingertips trail over the stubble on Trace's jawline. My mind told me he was a kid, but his body and the way he carried himself so confidently—knowing what he wanted and exactly how to get it—was so damn masculine.

"Don't start something you have no intention of finishing," Trace's gravelly voice warned.

"Just one more minute," I breathed.

"One more minute and I'll throw you over my shoulder and carry you upstairs."

A ripple rolled through my stomach. I believed he'd do it. I believed everything he said. He'd given me no reason not to. But I was getting in over my head. And regardless of how good he felt…and smelled…and looked, I dropped my hand and twisted away, rushing into the living room. "You should leave."

"Leave?" Trace followed me into the room carrying the beers and opener. "I thought things were just getting good."

I stopped at the front door with my hand on the knob. "Good?"

Ignoring me, he walked to the sofa and dropped down onto it. "Come sit with me."

"I don't think that's a good idea."

"Why?" He opened the bottles then glanced up at me. "Can't you trust yourself with me?"

"It's *you* I don't trust," I assured him.

He laughed. "I'm not gonna touch you until I know you're ready."

"What do you call what just happened in the kitchen?"

"That was me making sure you knew where I stood."

I shook my head at the absurdity of the whole situation. And only because I looked ridiculous standing at the door did I move to the love seat opposite where he sat on the sofa.

"Uh-uh." He patted the spot beside him.

I wanted to stand my ground. To keep my distance. To be stronger. But my resolve was seriously waning when it came to Trace. And, shamelessly, I moved toward him, grabbing one of the beers and taking a long swallow before I sat down beside him.

Not only was I in the middle of a divorce, I was becoming a lush and serving a teenager alcohol. Forget hell, I was going to jail.

An awkward silence descended as we both sat there drinking our beers. What was I supposed to say now that I'd just stepped over some pretty major lines?

"I miss him too," Trace said, breaking the uncomfortable silence.

My eyes cut to his.

"And if it's any consolation, you still have me."

I rolled my eyes. "Says the guy who's leaving town soon."

"Not for another month."

Exactly. A month and I'd be a distant memory. He'd be back on campus. He'd be traveling for football. He'd have his choice of girls. *Girls.*

"A lot can happen in a month," he said, and it sounded a lot like a promise.

I swallowed around the dryness in my throat as another silence descended upon us.

"I was serious when I said I want you to bring CJ to my home games."

I nodded, knowing I wouldn't hold him to it, but it was nice of him to offer.

"I get family seats right up front. I want to be able to see you guys cheering me on."

I tipped back my beer, wondering how that would work. His mother would just love having me there so she could grill me for more information to pass on to her friends. "Do we have to wear your jersey?"

He laughed. "And paint my number on your cheeks." He reached over and brushed his thumb over my cheek, igniting a path of tingles.

"We could do that," I said, trying to steady any chance of a quiver in my voice.

"I don't want you getting jealous. There might be quite a few girls with my number on their bodies."

I scoffed. "I think I can handle it."

He raised his brows as he slid his arm around the back of the sofa and dropped his hand on my shoulder, easing me into him. "Come here."

I rested my head on his shoulder, relishing in the way it felt.

"So, what are we gonna do while CJ's away?"

I closed my eyes on a sigh. How did he always know? How did he always know the right thing to say, and exactly what I needed? Charles never knew. He never considered me. I could see that clearer than ever with Trace in our lives.

"He never let me drink beer."

"What?"

"Charles. He never let me drink beer."

He pulled back and looked me in the eyes, disbelief written in his features. "No shit?"

"Nope. He said wine was more sophisticated."

"What an asshole."

"He never let me eat in bed," I continued.

Trace balked at the ridiculousness that had become my life.

"Or jump on the bed. CJ and I used to do it just to tease him and he wouldn't even crack a smile. Can you believe that?"

"I can't believe him not wanting to have fun with his wife and son."

I pulled in a deep breath. How had I been so blind? How had I settled? "Oh, and he hated ice cream. Who hates ice cream?"

"A douchebag."

I laughed.

"What the hell were you doing with him?"

"I have no idea."

* * *

My eyes cracked open. Sunlight filtered into my living room through my front window blinds. I jolted up. The blanket that somehow ended up on me dropped to the floor. My head twisted around my living room. My *empty* living room.

A mortified pit formed in the deep recesses of my stomach. What had I done? What had I let happen? What had I been thinking touching Trace?

His words came rushing back at me all at once. I'd been in his fantasies. I dropped my face into my palms. *Oh my freaking God.* What woman wouldn't be flattered by that? Yep. That's what made me touch him. It was the only reason I would've done it.

The hum of a lawnmower floated into my living room. It was close by. *Really* close by. I stood and walked to my French doors, peeking out at my backyard. A shirtless Trace pushed a lawnmower in perfect lines from one side of my yard to the other. *Talk about a lawn boy fantasy.* As if he heard my thoughts, his head turned and our eyes locked. I shrugged, as if to ask what he was doing. A cool smile slipped across his lips and he held up his finger. I glanced around, realizing he was just about done.

I walked back over to the sofa and dropped down, wondering what the hell I'd say to him now that the darkness was gone and all we had was the clarity of sunlight.

Outside, the hum of the mower switched off and Trace's footsteps resounded up the deck steps. "Morning," he said as he pulled open the door.

"You didn't have to mow my lawn."

He wiped off his grass covered feet before walking into the living room. "I wanted to."

My eyes zoned in on his shirtless chest. God, it was even better in broad daylight. I just wanted to touch it before I went to hell. Just once.

"Marin?"

My eyes jumped to his.

His easy smile told me he liked me looking. But as the adult in the room, I knew better.

I shook my head to somehow clear my thoughts. "Did you sleep here?"

He crossed his arms. "I did."

Sudden fear grabbed hold of me. How much had I drunk? Did I pass out or fall asleep?

He stifled a smile, though I could see the wheels turning as they played out across his face.

"What?" I asked.

"I was just wondering how long I can go on making you think something happened before I have to tell you the truth."

"And what's the truth?"

"I slept right there." He pointed to the loveseat.

A breath whooshed out of me.

"Relief is definitely not the reaction I get from only sleeping at a girl's place."

I cocked my head. "Probably because there's not a lot of sleeping going on."

He laughed. "Okay, so maybe I don't struggle getting girls' attention." He paused. "Except maybe one girl's."

Quivers hit me deep in my core. "Don't."

"Don't what?"

I closed my eyes, needing to resist his damn charm while not looking at him shirtless and sweaty in my living room. "Don't make me feel things."

"What kind of things?"

"Things I haven't felt since I was a teenager."

"Isn't that a good thing?"

I opened my eyes, unable to tell up from down with him in my house. In my space. In my head.

He ticked his head toward the front door. "You want me to go?"

"I don't know what I want." I scrubbed my hands up and down my face as if that would bring me some clarity. "I almost can't be trusted when you're around."

His face lit up. "I like where this is going."

Exasperation emanated off me. "It's not going anywhere."

"But it could," he countered.

"And I could be arrested."

"Stop it, Marin." His voice became annoyed. "I'm legal. I'm a senior in college, not high school."

"What are you even doing here? You have girls lined up for you. *Girls.* Not some lonely mother whose husband cheated on her."

His eyes narrowed on mine. "That's not what I see when I see you."

A humorless laugh shot out of me. "Well you should."

He walked over to the front door and grabbed the doorknob, his sudden change in demeanor disconcerting. "I'm gonna leave you alone with this pity party you've decided to throw yourself." His eyes brimmed with disappointment as he stared across the room at me. "The Marin I've gotten to know is tougher than this."

I threw my hands up. "Oh, great. Now the neighbors are gonna see you sneaking out of my house."

"Nope. They'll see me walking out the door in no particular rush. Because I know what I want. It's you who needs to figure it out."

He pulled open the door and walked out leaving me feeling like the pathetic fool I was.

CHAPTER NINE

Marin

I tossed a bag of chips into my shopping cart, moving on to the cookie aisle to grab CJ's favorite sandwich cookies so I'd have them when he returned. My phone pinged in my handbag. I pulled it out and checked the text. **You done being a wuss?**

I huffed my frustration and dropped the phone back into my handbag, continuing down the aisle.

"Hi, Marin."

I turned my head in the direction of the voice. One of the moms from CJ's camp approached. I glanced into her cart. It was filled with fruits and vegetables. I glanced in mine. It was filled with junk food, soda, and juice. Ah, well. "Hi, Cheryl."

"Is CJ getting excited for kindergarten?" she asked, all bright eyed and fresh from her daily yoga class.

"I think so. How about Greta?"

She laughed. "She already had me buy all the supplies on the list they sent home. She can't wait for school to start."

My phone pinged in my handbag. I pulled it out as Cheryl continued to talk about Greta and all her extra-curricular activities. **I want to see you.**

I began to shove the phone back in my handbag when it pinged again. I didn't want to look but I couldn't stop myself. **Why are you so scared of me?**

"Marin? Did you hear me?" Cheryl asked.

I shoved the phone in my bag. "I'm sorry. What did you say?"

She continued on for the next fifteen minutes about the best teachers to get and the PTA moms to steer clear of as my phone continued to ping in my handbag.

* * *

Television lights flashed across my dark living room. Gayle and I were cozied up under a blanket on my sofa and had just binge-watched every chick flick we could find.

"Ugh," I said as the happy couple on screen kissed in the rain after declaring their undying love for one another.

Gayle bumped me with her shoulder. "Stop being such a downer."

"Movies like this make girls believe life is all about kisses in the rain. It's not."

Gayle shook her head. "You, my friend, need to get back out there. Just because you married an asshole doesn't mean you won't meet someone who isn't."

"Where? At the supermarket? In line to pick up CJ from school? Nice guys are married and the single ones are single for a reason." *Like they're too young.*

"Listen, I was the only one who warned you about Charles. I knew he was a stiff. I knew you were too good for him. Too fun for him. But you didn't listen. So why are you *still* not listening to me? I'm wise beyond my years. I know things. I'm intuitive."

I rolled my eyes. "You're something all right."

She laughed.

A knock on the front door caused our eyes to dart to it.

"You expecting someone?" Gayle asked.

"No."

Suddenly eager—too eager—to see who stood on the other side of the door, Gayle jumped to her feet and hurried to it.

"Tell me you didn't hire me a stripper," I groaned.

She threw back her long dark curls and howled with laughter. "No, but thanks for the idea."

"Wait—"

She didn't, throwing the door wide open. Her eyes rounded and a huge grin lit up her face.

"Hi." Trace's deep voice trailed in from the front step. "Is Marin here?"

My body buzzed at the sound of his voice. Recollections of his hands on me flooded my brain. *Dammit.*

"Holy shit," Gayle said unapologetically, her eyes shifting to mine. "You didn't tell me he was this hot in person."

Trace stepped inside, a shit-eating grin on his face as his eyes found me on the sofa. "Oh, no?" He glanced back to Gayle who'd shut the door and was examining every inch of him like something she planned to eat. "What *did* she tell you?"

I stared Gayle down, hating her for opening the door and for her none-too-subtle gawking.

"Oh, you know. Girl stuff," she said. "What brings you over?"

I could have died. I could have crawled up into a ball and died right there. Could she not play it cool?

Trace looked to me. "Why didn't you respond to my texts?"

"You texted?" I feigned surprise.

He stared at me, his narrowed eyes unconvinced.

"I didn't check my phone. Gayle and I were having a girls' night."

"But now it's over." Gayle reached for her sweatshirt from the chair and threw it on, slipping her feet into her flip-flops as she did.

"No," I said to her through gritted teeth.

She shrugged at Trace. "Sorry I can't stay and chat." The damn traitor winked at me before disappearing out the door.

"She was nice," Trace said.

"Yep." I jumped to my feet and grabbed our empty glasses and plates and took off for the kitchen.

"So, why don't you tell me why you really didn't respond," he said, following me into the kitchen.

"Because this is silly." I placed the glasses and plates on the counter.

"What is?"

I spun around to face him, frustration taking hold of me. "Us."

"I didn't realize there was an *us*. There's me trying to get you to hang out with me and you wussing out."

"I'm not wussing out."

"Prove it." He moved closer, his eyes locked on mine as I took a step back slamming into the counter behind me.

Instead of wincing at the pain now emanating in my back or the unwavering look in his eyes, my body trembled with desire.

His hands landed on my hips, strong and possessive. "Show me your room."

My heart drummed faster. My eyes fixed on his. "What?"

"Show me your room, Marin."

"Stop." The word barely came out.

"I can't."

I could feel my resolve weakening as I stared into his eyes. "When will you be twenty?"

The pulse in his jaw ticked as he grasped me tighter. "We're not waiting."

"When?" I demanded, hoping it would somehow relieve the trepidation racing through my brain.

"November third."

"Fuuuuck," I hissed under my breath.

But the word was cut off by his mouth crashing down on mine. Our lips collided in an explosion of need. Want. Desire. He may have been the one pursuing me, but I couldn't resist him any longer. I wrapped my arms around his neck. My body arched into him as his tongue pushed inside my mouth, holding me prisoner while it tangled with mine. Trace lowered his hands to my ass, lifting me effortlessly. I wrapped my legs around his hips as he spun me around, slamming my back against the refrigerator. The glass inside clanked loudly. The friction of our bodies and the pressure of his chest right where I needed it did little to ease the throbbing between my thighs. I moved my hips, rubbing shamelessly against him as he devoured my lips. I pulled back breathless. "Upstairs. My room's upstairs."

Trace spun me away from the refrigerator and carried me across the kitchen and up the stairs, his eyes never leaving mine. I could see the pent-up frustration. Hell, I could feel it. Once he found my room, he made a beeline toward my bed. His knees hit the foot of it and he tossed me down.

My body bounced on my white down comforter. Pillows tumbled to the floor. I propped myself up on my elbows with my chest heaving, taking in the vision of him standing at the foot of my bed. The sliver of light from the hallway provided the only light in my otherwise dark room.

Never in my wildest dreams had I ever envisioned this scenario playing out. Never had I envisioned anyone other than Charles in this room. And never someone so young staring at me like he wanted to do very bad things to me.

Trace reached behind his head, grabbing the neck of his shirt and pulling it off. My eyes explored those cavernous ridges and dips in his chest. Not one to be shy, he pushed his jeans and boxers down his legs, giving me my own private strip tease.

My breath hitched as I drank him in. Forget the bare chest, it had been some time since I'd seen a naked guy. And this one was the perfect male specimen. Trace's lips tipped up in the corners as he stood there all confident and perfect, letting me appreciate him. Letting me admire what he'd been given and was ready to give me.

Unable to take the distance any longer, I crooked my index finger toward me. My body whirred with a mix of need and indecision as his smile grew. He slowly approached, crawling on top of me and easing me onto my back. I pushed the fears from my head as his eyes dropped to my mouth. If his mere look could elicit such want, I couldn't imagine what having him inside me would do.

He lowered his mouth to mine. His kiss was slow and intoxicating as his body began moving over me. He wanted more but was giving me time to let it happen. He wasn't going to push me. Or rush me. He was going to milk the time with me, teasing me with a taste of the pleasure he had to offer.

My hands slipped around his hips, my fingers trailing over his smooth back. His skin was silk under my hands, his solid muscles beneath such a stark contrast. I moved my fingertips down to the dip above his ass, palming his ass as he continued to move above me.

Trace pulled back, staring down at me with dilated pupils and labored breaths. "I want to see you, Marin. All of you this time."

My belly dipped at the rasp in his voice and the desperate look in his eyes. My trembling hands reached for the hem of my shirt. Trace sat back on his knees, his eyes ready to take me in. I peeled the fabric over my head, hearing the catch in his breath as I discarded it on the floor. There was a heady feeling knowing how desired I was in that moment.

"You have no idea what this is like," Trace said, as he leaned over me, easing me back.

My brows inverted. "What?"

"Having your fantasy come to life."

I closed my eyes, shaking my head at the awe in his voice and the fear that awe elicited in me. "I'm afraid I'll disappoint you."

He brushed his thumb over my cheek. "You've already exceeded all my expectations and I haven't even been inside you yet."

The throbbing between my thighs intensified. "That's what I'm afraid of."

He slipped down my body, his nose tunneling between my breasts.

I dropped my head back on the pillow as his lips pressed open-mouth kisses down to my stomach. I squeezed my eyes shut, the sensations already too much to bear.

This was happening.

This was really freaking happening.

Could he feel my heart jumping out of my chest?

His tongue shot out, swiping a path around my navel. My belly quivered. The rest of my body following suit. My sensitive skin became hyper aware of how bare I was and how his mere touch ignited a fire everywhere.

"I spent so many nights alone in my room thinking of you," he murmured against my skin. "What you'd feel like. What you'd taste like. What you'd sound like when I made you come."

I groaned as he kissed a path back up my stomach, his tongue shooting out and tasting the underside of my breast. Lightheadedness overtook me. I wasn't used to this type of foreplay. I'd forgotten how amazing it could be. I grasped the sides of Trace's head, guiding his mouth over my nipple. He took it between his lips, sucking with just the right pressure to make my eyes cross. The back of my head pressed deeper into my pillow as he bit down gently, tempering the sting with the pressure of his tongue. "Oh, God," I gasped.

He smiled against my skin. "Every. Damn. Time." He moved to my other breast, continuing the same glorious torture.

I kept myself centered, focusing on every sensation his mouth awakened. It was like he knew just what to do and when to do it. I could barely catch my breath before he descended, his hands coasting over my sides as he kissed his way back down to my navel. But this time he didn't stop. He gripped the sides of my shorts and pulled them down, taking my underwear with them. I dragged in a deep breath as he moved lower, inhaling as he passed the crux between my legs. "Smells fucking amazing."

I draped my arm across my eyes as he tossed my remaining clothes to the floor. His possessive hands parted my thighs. I pulled in a sharp breath as he buried his face between them. He didn't hesitate. His tongue shot out, licking a path up my seam, back to front, pushing on my clit with pulsing beats. I whimpered, unable to hold back as he repeated the same glorious torture over and over again.

"You taste so good," he said before his tongue thrust deep between my folds.

Shamelessly I moaned, finally understanding the meaning of ecstasy. Because Trace between my legs—making me feel more worshipped than I'd ever felt in my life—felt so. Damn. Good. "Don't stop."

"Not going anywhere," he murmured, the vibration against my skin causing my eyes to pinch tighter. He returned to my clit, sucking it between his lips and moving it slowly back and forth. As if that sensation wasn't enough, he flattened his tongue and pressed on it, then flicked it relentlessly.

Oh. My. Freaking. God.

I couldn't take the pleasure. It was all too much. All too intense. My body coiled, all the tension amassing in that tiny spot filled with so many glorious nerve endings. One last suck and flick sent me toppling over the edge of reason, plummeting into a vicious spiral. My breath rushed out of me all at once as my chest heaved.

Trace slid back up my body, stopping when he hovered over me wearing the smuggest smirk I'd ever seen. I wanted to lick the dimples that dug into his cheeks. Instead, I savored the buzz of my body. The weight of him over me. The lust in his eyes.

"That's what I hoped you'd sound like." He buried his face in the side of my neck, assailing my skin with open-mouthed kisses. His hand drifted down my body to the now sensitive skin between my legs. Two fingers slipped inside me, slowly pushing in and out, seeking any rogue tremors. "I could do this all night long," he murmured.

My eyes widened. There was no way I had the stamina he had, especially since it had been so long.

"Making you feel good is quickly becoming my favorite thing to do," he continued.

Both flattered and afraid, I released a sigh. To keep this thing between us casual—to keep either one of us from thinking it was something it wasn't—we both needed to benefit. "Let me make *you* feel good." My throaty voice sounded nothing like my own.

"You already are," he said as he dropped slow kisses up and down my collarbone.

I pushed on his chest, trying to shift his weight off me. He took the hint, withdrawing his fingers and rolling onto his back with me clinging to him. Bare skin to bare skin we were a perfect match. I didn't want to lose the contact. Didn't want to lose his solid body beneath mine. Because in that moment, it was just Trace and Marin.

Nothing else existed.

Trace reached off the side of the bed and dug into the pocket of his jeans, returning with a condom. I pulled it from him and sat on his thighs. He locked his arms behind his head, his biceps bulging as he relished in the sight of me naked on top of him. His heavy-lidded eyes confirmed his claims. He *had* wanted this with me. I tore open the package and rolled the condom on him. His eyes zeroed in on my fingers. "God, that feels good."

I pressed my hands into the mattress on either side of Trace's head and leaned down. His erection pressed to my belly as I buried my lips in the side of his neck. I dragged my tongue up from his collarbone to the soft skin beneath his ear, latching playfully onto his earlobe and tugging gently.

"Oh, fuck. I'm not gonna be able to keep my hands to myself," he growled as his hands dropped to my ass, his fingers digging into my flesh.

I continued sucking away at his skin as I aligned myself with his straining erection. My wet skin drifted over the length of him, just shy of letting him inside. Back and forth. Hitting the tender spot he'd worshipped so thoroughly over and over again.

His head flew off the pillow as his hands shifted and grasped hold of my hips. "Are you trying to kill me?"

I sat up with a grin and he wasted no time. His hands guided my hips until I hovered over him. I lowered myself slowly, adjusting to the size of him as I sank to the hilt.

Gahhh.

Trace's head dropped back, his eyes squeezing shut. "Holy fuck."

I rocked my hips, lifting them then sinking back down. Once I found my rhythm, his teeth clenched and moans resonated from the back of his throat. He cracked his eyes and watched me, his focus dropping to where we were connected. "You feel so much better than my hand ever did."

My head dropped forward, my hair falling over my shoulders as my eyes drifted to where his gaze was locked. In the morning, I might've regretted the decision to sleep with him, but right then, right when everything felt exactly the way it should, I had no regrets. I followed my heart for once in my life and ignored my head. And holy Jesus it felt so good.

Trace's breathing became ragged as one of his hands drifted from my hip to where our bodies were joined. His thumb brushed over my throbbing clit. I sat up straighter as my head fell back, my hair draped down my back as my rhythm became faster and more intense. The pressure of his thumb intensified too. In one fell swoop my body tightened around him. Trembles fired out in every direction. And even though I wanted to stop to catch my breath and savor the glorious feelings spreading over me, I continued moving, wanting to bring Trace to that place. Wanting him to feel how good I could make it for him. Wanting to live up to his expectations.

It didn't take long. His hands gripped my hips so tightly he surely left bruises. His features tightened and his body stilled.

Watching it happen was almost as satisfying as feeling it happen. So I kept moving until every last bit of pleasure was wrung from his body. When it was, I lowered myself to his heaving chest, leaving him pulsing inside me.

He wrapped his arms around me and pressed his lips to the top of my head. "I have no words."

I laughed, feeling the exact same way as my own sweaty body fought to come back down to Earth.

"I'm serious. How do you convey what it feels like to get something you've wanted for so long?"

"Stop exaggerating."

He grabbed the sides of my head and lifted it gently so my chin rested on his chest. "Marin, don't you get it? When I was a teenager alone with my hand, it was you I imagined."

"You're still a teenager," I reminded him.

"Not many teenagers can make you feel the way I did."

I chewed on my bottom lip, wanting to tell him most *men* couldn't make me feel the way he did.

"There are times I'm with other girls and it's you I envision beneath me," he said. "You moaning. You breathing my name."

Feeling too awkward to look at him, I dropped my forehead onto his chest. "You didn't even know me."

"I knew your smile and your laugh. You just exuded happiness anytime you were around. I just wanted to be caught up in it. I wanted to feel it. Touch it. Touch you." He gently lifted my face again. "I was paying attention all those years, Marin. And now that I know you, you're everything I thought you'd be."

I rolled my eyes at the absurdity of his words. Of our situation.

"You're strong and compassionate and an amazing mother." His lips twisted into that smirk that brought on eager butterflies. "And you're so damn sexy you don't even realize it."

I shook my head, my eyes averting his.

"So, thank you," he said.

I glanced back to him. "For what?"

"For proving me right. And for giving us a chance." The gentleness of his subsequent kiss conveyed the sincerity of his words and feelings.

It was me who wasn't as confident in the *us* he referred to. It was sex. Amazing, toe curling sex. But he was still leaving for school. And I was still a mother without a job.

CHAPTER TEN

Marin

My body was still tangled with Trace's when the early morning sun cracked through my closed bedroom blinds. I could say with much certainty I hadn't slept so soundly in years. Unfortunately, now that I lay awake, my mind taunted me with all the reasons why the previous night had been a terrible idea. All the reasons this thing with Trace needed to end immediately.

I sat up slowly, careful not to wake Trace as I tugged the sheet from our feet and wrapped it around my naked body. I glanced down at him. The scarce sunlight cast a soft glow over him stretched out on my bed. Naked. Sound asleep. Hair all ruffled. Looking right at home.

I needed to breathe and I didn't need to see him sprawled out on my bed while I did. I stood, tiptoeing toward my bathroom.

"Where are you going?" Trace's raspy morning voice asked.

I stopped and closed my eyes. Heat crept up my neck. It was one thing to have sex with him at night, in the darkness, but now that it was morning, it wasn't so easy to face him. Pulling in a long breath, I glanced over my shoulder. "Oh, I…"

Trace pushed himself up onto his elbows. "Stop."

"Stop what?"

"Stop trying to sneak out of here."

I hugged the sheet tighter around me and turned to face him. "That's not what I was doing."

"Bullshit."

I huffed. "Why do you have to challenge me?"

"Because I can." He crawled toward me, kneeling on the edge of the bed. "Now come here."

I tilted my head, my brain wanting to resist him, but my heart…my stupid heart couldn't shake the sight of him naked on my bed. Or the pleading look in his eyes. Or the way he made me feel.

Gahhhh.

I stepped to him. He wrapped his arms around me, pulling me tightly against the solid plains of his chest. His aloe scent I'd been inhaling all night, encompassed me in a real-life cocoon. And his body—his amazing body—overwhelmed every one of my senses. The ache between my legs returned with a vengeance. Trace slipped his hand inside the sheet, releasing it from my body. It dropped to the floor and pooled around my feet. "I need you, Marin."

I pulled my head back and stared into his eyes. "I don't want to need *you.*"

He stared back at me. He wanted to say something. I could see it in the way his eyes riveted between mine. In the way his mouth opened then pressed together in a tight line. His hands slid up my bare back. Goosebumps erupted in their wake. "Until CJ comes home, I want to be the first face you see in the morning and the last one you see before you close your eyes."

How could I argue with that?

Regardless of the reasons it was a bad idea, I went willingly. I needed to savor my time with Trace. I'd learned from what happened with Charles—how I'd lost such a huge piece of myself—that I needed to enjoy life. And Trace, for a growing number of reasons, made me happier than I'd been in a long time.

Trace

The walk of shame had never felt as sweet as it did after spending one hell of a night in Marin's bed. I actually took the time to appreciate the trees lining the sidewalk, their green leaves waiting patiently to be replaced with vibrant reds and oranges. And while fall made most people think of pumpkins and scarecrows, for this Bama boy it was all about football. Football was my life eighty percent of the year. That's why I felt like I was being a selfish prick when it came to Marin. I was leaving. I'd be back at school in less than a month and have no time for anything but classes and football. But I just couldn't help myself.

I twisted the knob on the side door of my parents' house. It was unlocked, which meant my disappearing act the previous night hadn't gone unnoticed. I slipped inside the kitchen, careful not to make a sound as I closed the door and moved to the fridge. I grabbed the container of orange juice and tipped it down my throat, needing sustenance after the workout I'd had with Marin.

"Nice of you to come home." My mother's voice was like nails on a chalkboard.

I replaced the orange juice and closed the fridge, turning slowly.

My mother stood in the doorway with her robe knotted tightly at the waist and her disapproving glare fixed firmly in place. "Would it kill you to leave a note or text to let us know you'll be out all night?"

At school I had no one to answer to. It was easy to forget I had parents who worried while I was home. "Sorry. It just kinda happened."

She slipped a chair out from the kitchen table and sat, primed for her typical interrogation. "Do you plan on telling me where you were?"

"I'd rather not."

She nodded, clearly pissed. "And if I already know?"

I crossed my arms and leaned against the center island. "Then you already know."

"And if I think it's a terrible idea?"

I shrugged. "Then you think it's a terrible idea."

"So, my opinion means nothing to you?"

"I appreciate you looking out for me. But I can make my own decisions. Just like I can make my own mistakes. I'm a man now."

"Then start acting like one," she said, her harsh tone taking me aback.

"Excuse me?"

"You heard me. The way you've been carrying on with her is despicable." Her face scrunched in distaste which pissed *me* the hell off.

"First of all, she has a name and you know it. Second, we're friends."

"Friends?" she sneered. "That's what they're calling it these days?"

"I don't like what you're implying."

"I'm not implying anything. She's a single mother. She has no business latching on to you."

"Latching on to me?" My voice was incredulous.

"She asked you to spend time with her son."

"Right. She *asked* me and I could've said no."

"Why didn't you?"

"Because, despite what you think, I enjoy having a little kid around who wants nothing more than to hang out with me and emulate me. And he's an awesome kid."

"And what about her?"

My head dropped back and I dragged in a breath. "I like her. She got the short end of the stick with that asshole she married."

"I won't condone this."

"I'm not asking you to."

"What if the scouts find out?"

"Find out what?"

She shook her head, a snare on her lips. "You're still a teenager for Christ's sake."

"For a few more months."

She threw her hands in the air. "Logistics."

"What happened to you supporting me?"

"I do support you," she snapped.

"Then start acting like it." I pushed off the island and walked out of the kitchen.

CHAPTER ELEVEN

Marin

I miss you.

Trace's text came during his shift at the bar. It had been hours since he'd dragged himself from my bed. Once he had, I lay in bed with his scent still clinging to my sheets replaying our night in my head. I couldn't actually remember ever being that worshipped. That content. That happy.

I sent back a text. **Oh, yeah? What do you miss?**
Your bed.
I laughed to myself.
Your taste.
My belly rippled.
Your sounds.

Oh, he was good. But what did I expect? The guy had moves I never imagined I'd be on the receiving end of.

The way your body does whatever I want it to do.
Okay. This did not help. **What are you doing after work?**
You.

I tossed my phone down on the coffee table like a hot potato. I was in over my head. The guy had sexting down to a science. How many girls had been the lucky recipients of his texts? Actually, it was probably better I didn't know.

I picked up my laptop and continued researching graduate programs at the local colleges—something I'd been doing all night. I needed to get back in the game. I couldn't do anything in my field without a Master's degree. I already had twelve credits, having taken four classes before Charles asked me to stop. I could manage the ten remaining classes, practicums, and internship if I worked my butt off for the next two years.

My phone rang, pulling me from my search. I grabbed it and lifted it to my ear.

"Why haven't you called?" Gayle asked before I could even speak.

"What do you mean?"

"Girl, I left you with the hottest guy I've ever seen and you have the nerve not to call. I should've been the first call after he left."

"What if he didn't leave?"

Her scream was so loud I needed to hold the phone away from my ear.

"Are you done?" I laughed.

"Is he still there?" she managed to ask once she finally calmed down.

"No."

"I can't believe you tapped that."

"I don't think anyone says that anymore."

"I don't care what they say, tell me everything. I need to live through you. Sam has a beer gut."

I sat back and sighed, the visions still so fresh. So raw. "It was freaking incredible."

Her envious screech carried through the phone until I heard Sam burst into the room asking if she was okay. "Yes, I'm fine," she told him. "Marin's tapping her hot neighbor."

"Gayle," I hissed.

"Oh, relax. Who's he gonna tell?"

"I just don't want people to know."

"Why the hell not? If a hot guy wanted to sleep with me, I'd want the whole world to know—sorry, honey."

I laughed to myself as she apologized to her husband.

"Is he coming over tonight?" she asked.

"I think so."

"This couldn't have happened to a better person."

"I didn't win an award. I'm sleeping with my nineteen-year-old neighbor."

"There is nothing teen about him, Marin. He is *all* man—"

Sam growled in the background.

"Oh, relax," she said to him.

I laughed. "I'll let you go before you end up sleeping alone tonight."

"I couldn't get that lucky," she said.

* * *

Soft knocking on the front door woke me from the vivid dream I'd been having on the sofa. I glanced to my phone. It was 11:15 p.m. Right on time. I dragged my fingers through my matted hair and made my way to the front door, eagerly pulling it open.

Trace stood there in cargo shorts and a navy shirt with a backpack on his back. He looked so damn fine I just stared at him, knowing he was there for me and only me. "Hi."

He said nothing, just stepped into me so I had to back up. He closed the door behind him and wrapped his arms around me, staring down at me with those pretty blue eyes. I yearned for him to kiss me. To touch me. To something. "I like when you look at me," he said, his voice deep yet vulnerable.

"Oh, yeah?"

He nodded. "It makes me feel like you see me."

"Of course I see you."

His hands lifted to my cheeks, his fingertips lightly brushing my hair back from my face. "All those years when I went out of my way to pass by here just to see you, you barely even looked at me."

"You were a kid."

His lips tipped up in one corner. "Yeah. But don't you get it? I've always seen you, Marin. All those years. And it's just crazy to finally have you looking back and seeing me."

I lifted my hands to his face, my fingertips gliding over the stubble around his jawline. "I like seeing you." My fingers slipped to the back of his head, drawing his mouth to mine. Though he came willingly, I controlled the kiss, trying to convey how much I saw him. How much I wanted him there. How willing I was to give this thing between us a chance.

His tongue slid inside my mouth, and instantly he'd taken over. I knew it wouldn't take long. I loved his possessive nature, especially when it was directed at me. He stopped the kiss way too soon and stepped back, pulling his backpack from his back.

I eyed it with a lifted brow. "Planning on staying?"

He smirked. "I don't need clothes for that. Do me a favor. Meet me upstairs."

My brows inverted.

He snickered. "I'll make it worth your while."

"Okay." I moved toward the stairs, glancing over my shoulder at him standing there watching me.

"Go ahead. I wanna watch that fine ass."

My body shuddered as his eyes drifted to my butt. Suddenly eager for what he had planned, I hurried up the stairs and disappeared into my room. As I sat on the edge of my bed waiting, I could hear the cabinets and drawers opening and closing down in the kitchen.

Trace's footsteps soon resounded up the stairs. When my bedroom door swung open, he stood there holding bowls and utensils with his backpack dangling from his forearm. He moved to the bed and placed his bag down, moving the bowls and utensils to the nightstand.

"What's all this?"

He dug into his backpack and pulled out a container of chocolate ice cream followed by a container of vanilla and held them up. "I wasn't sure which flavor you liked."

My eyes narrowed. "Ice cream?"

He stacked the containers on my nightstand then pulled chocolate sprinkles, hot fudge, and whipped cream out of his bag. "Not just ice cream. Everything you need to make an ice cream sundae. In bed."

I stared back at him, realizing what he'd done. He'd listened when I talked. He'd heard what I'd said about Charles. He knew the life I'd lived, and he was trying to show me what life should've been like. The only problem was I was starting to see what life with *him* could be like, and that scared the hell out of me. "Thank you."

He shrugged like it was no big deal. But it was.

"Chocolate," I said.

He smiled as he grabbed the chocolate container and sat beside me. "Good choice."

As he peeled off the cover, I reached over and grabbed the hot fudge and whipped cream. He laughed as I squeezed a big glob of fudge on top of the ice cream then piled a mountain of whipped cream on top of it. I picked up one of the spoons and dug into the carton, savoring the taste of it as soon as it touched my tongue.

"Good?" he asked as I dug back in, getting another big spoonful.

"You tell me." I stood up and moved in front of him. He stared up at me, awaiting my next move. I stepped forward and straddled his lap. He smiled as I lifted the spoon to his lips. He opened his mouth and ate the ice cream off my spoon. Given the erection straining in his shorts and the way he stared right back at me as he savored his bite, he liked me there. "Is this one of your fantasies?" I asked.

He leaned forward, and with chocolate coating his tongue, he kissed me. He kissed me hard, his tongue exploring my mouth, deliciously stroking against my tongue. When he pulled out of the kiss, he moved the ice cream to the nightstand. "No." He grabbed the bottle of whipped cream and lifted the spout to my mouth. "But this is," he said, all sexy and raspy.

I opened slightly, wanting to play along and make his fantasy a reality. He squirted a small dab inside my mouth, and before I could close it, his mouth was on mine, his tongue swiping the whipped cream out as he sucked away at my tongue. The mix of ice cream and whipped cream was a heady combination, as was his erection pressing between my thighs.

Trace reclined on the bed, pulling me down on top of him. I giggled as our mouths came apart for a second before they were like magnets colliding, our lips moving rhythmically together. I reached for his hand and took the bottle, pulling back breathless. "My turn."

His dimples dug in before he opened his mouth. I lifted the spout, enjoying him anticipating my next move too much to actually do it. "Come on," he laughed.

I moved the spout a couple inches to the right and squirted a dollop onto his dimple, licking it away as he snickered. I moved to the left side and did the same. "I love your dimples."

"Oh yeah?"

I nodded. "I'm a sucker for dimples. Now open."

He did and I shot the whipped cream onto his tongue, leaning down and licking away at the inside of his mouth, relishing in the ease of being in Trace's arms.

He grabbed hold of me and rolled me onto my back, pulling the bottle from my hand.

"I wasn't finished yet," I demanded.

"Neither was I." He pointed the bottle at the side of my neck and squirted a path down to my collarbone. The cold cream on my warm skin sent goosebumps scrambling up my arms and legs. He leaned down and, with a slow tortuous drag of his tongue, he licked his way from my collarbone to my ear, ridding my skin of the cream.

My body trembled. The anticipation of what the rest of our night would be like was overpowering.

I reached for the bottle, but Trace shook his head. "Uh, uh." He moved the bottle to the other side of my neck, squirting a similar path down to my collarbone. Again, he leaned down and dragged his tongue slowly over my skin, collecting it all before returning to my mouth and kissing me hard.

I was drowning in the feel of him. In the feelings his kiss elicited. In the way he made me want to live.

The bottle rolled loose from his hand and landed with a thump on the carpet. He brought his hands up and tunneled them through my hair. "I need you naked."

"I need you naked."

He laughed, and when he laughed like that, all husky and real, it hit me deep. "Then we're in agreement."

I watched his eyes as they stayed on mine, just staring into them as if he could somehow hear my thoughts. Feel my emotions.

"And I need to feel you beneath me."

I swallowed hard as he yanked off his shirt. I would never get sick of looking at him. I lifted my hand and brushed my fingertips lightly over the smooth sculpted surface.

"You like?" he asked.

"God, yes."

He chuckled and reached for my top, peeling it off and discarding it on the floor with his.

"You like?" I teased, having removed my bra before I fell asleep earlier.

He smirked, before leaning down and taking my nipple between his lips.

Holy hell. My thighs quivered as my back arched, my head digging into my pillow. His cold mouth brought on sensations I wasn't expecting. I reached down and pushed at my shorts, needing to be rid of them and closer to him.

Trace smiled against my breast. "Don't worry. I've got you." He reached down and shoved my shorts and panties down my legs. I kicked them off the rest of the way. Trace reached for his own shorts and within seconds, they were gone and he'd tossed a condom beside my head. "Now, where was I?"

His mouth returned to my breast. The need within me intensified now that our naked bodies were nearly one. I lifted my hips, seeking comfort, but he ignored my pleas, continuing his delicious torture.

Knowing I wouldn't be able to take much more, I reached between us and grabbed hold of him. He stilled, his eyes pinching shut as my hand moved in a slow rhythm up and down. He gritted his teeth, his breathing becoming ragged as I continued my pursuit. I loved the feel of him in my hand. Loved the smooth skin and the solidity beneath it. Loved how powerful and in charge I felt.

Trace's hand shot out, grabbing the condom and tearing the wrapper with his teeth. "No way it's happening like this," he growled. I released him as he reached down and rolled it on. Then his mouth was on mine, devouring me as his erection ran along my slick skin. "I'm not gonna be able to be gentle," he said against my lips. "I've been thinking about you all fucking—"

My mouth cut him off, swallowing his words. He wasn't kidding. He braced his elbows beside my head and with one hard thrust pushed inside me. My back arched off the bed as my head slammed against my pillow. *Je-sus*. His weight on top of me this time made it all the more intense. Intimate. Real. He pulled away from my lips, his eyes dazed as his hips moved harder than I was used to. But I liked it. I liked everything he did.

My hands ran down his back, moving slowly over the hardened ridges of his muscles before landing on his ass. I dug my fingertips in as he moved in and out of me. I loved feeling him thrusting. Loved his grunts. Loved the way he leaned down and kissed me with sloppy wet kisses. I lifted my legs and linked them around his lower back. He moved faster. The throbbing between my legs slowly began to spiral. It was a matter of seconds before I'd uncoil. "Trace," I said breathless.

"I'm with you, Marin." He buried his face in the crook of my neck as he slammed into me.

And just like that, my body let go and powerful tremors shot down to my toes. Trace followed me over the edge, stilling above me as he dragged in long deep breaths that fanned onto my neck as he exhaled.

Slowly, he lowered himself down on top of me. "You're going to kill me, woman."

I laughed as his weight pressed me into the mattress. "That's called good sex."

He smiled against my skin as he wrapped his arms around me and rolled onto his side, with my sweaty body clinging to his. "I've had good sex. This is something else."

Oh, boy.

CHAPTER TWELVE

Marin

"Go out with me tonight," Trace said, his fingers trailing lightly up and down my arm draped over his chest.

"Where?" I asked, noticing the melted containers of ice cream on my nightstand.

"I have no fucking clue. I just want to spend time with you outside this house."

"Why?"

"Why the hell not?" He laughed. "I want to show you off."

I smiled at the honesty in his words.

My phone vibrated on the nightstand. Trace grabbed it and didn't even look at the screen before handing it to me. Charles would've checked *and* decided if I could talk to whomever it was or not. CJ's name lit up the screen. I sprang up, answering it immediately. "Hey, sweetie. Is everything okay?"

"I'm okay," CJ said, though nothing about his solemn tone convinced me.

Trace sat up, linking his hand with my free hand. "He okay?" he whispered.

I shrugged. "Where's Dad?"

"Don't know. Probably downstairs on the phone again."

"What'd you guys do yesterday?"

"He brought me to Grammy and Pop's."

"Were you with them all day?" I asked, even though I was fairly certain Charles ditched CJ with his parents.

"Yeah," CJ said, his voice soft and heartbreaking.

I was trying so hard to sound as if I didn't want to kill his father for not caring about him as much as I did. For not wanting to be with him all the time. For not being as amazing as Trace. "Well, I bet you had fun."

"It was okay," he said, but again I didn't believe him.

"What are you and Dad doing today?" I asked, trying to sound upbeat and excited for him.

"Not sure."

"Is there something you'd like to do? I can call him and suggest it."

"Well…I told him how me and Trace play basketball and football and asked if he wanted to, but he got kinda mad and said no."

Tears pricked my eyes. I wanted my little boy home and I wanted my ex to stay out of our lives for good. But how could I do that? How could I make it a reality? Charles was a lawyer for Christ's sake. If he didn't want me to have physical custody, I wouldn't.

"Can I talk to him?" Trace whispered.

I nodded, needing a minute to reign in my anger. "Oh honey," I said, trying to sound surprised. "Guess who just stopped by."

"Who?" CJ asked.

I handed the phone to Trace and he put it on speaker. "Hey, buddy."

CJ gasped. "Trace!"

"I miss you, buddy. I've got no one to play with."

"Mom can play with you."

Trace glanced to me with bouncing brows. "Tell you what. As soon as you get home, we're gonna do whatever you want to do. Basketball, football, baseball. You name it, we'll do it. How's that sound?"

"Really?" CJ asked, so hopeful and excited.

"You bet."

"How about fishing?"

"Absolutely."

"Thanks Trace. I love you."

My body froze. Tears no longer pricked my eyes but trailed down my cheeks. Rarely had I ever heard CJ tell Charles he loved him, but I could hear in his voice that he really meant it.

Trace glanced to me sadly. "I love you too, buddy."

"I better go before Dad catches me on the phone," CJ said.

"Okay," Trace and I said at the same time.

"Love you, CJ," I said.

"Love you more than the universe, Mom."

I disconnected the call. And before I could fall back onto the bed and lose myself in tears, Trace wrapped his arms around me and pulled me into him.

"He's gonna be fine, Marin. The douchebag's showing his true colors and CJ misses you like crazy."

I cried into his shoulder. "I just wish I could do something to make it better."

"You being strong for him is all you can do."

I nodded. "Thank you."

"You don't need to thank me, Marin. I want him home, too."

Trace

I stared across the candlelit table at Marin. No one ever would've believed she'd been brought to tears by her insensitive prick of an ex earlier that day. She'd been smiling and laughing, thoroughly enjoying my company all night. And don't even get me started on her sexy black dress.

"So, I'm going back to school," she said between bites of cheesecake.

"Yeah? That's great."

She nodded. "I signed up for two classes at The University of Mobile. I decided I want to get my Master's in Marriage and Family Counseling. I need ten more classes, two practicums, and an internship."

"You can get those done in two semesters," I assured her.

"I'm not going full time. It'll take me longer, with CJ and all. If I take two classes a semester and one or two during the summer, I should be able to have it done in two years. Maybe three."

It sucked that her ex asked her to stop going to school. Who does that? She would've already had her Master's.

"What are you thinking?" she asked, noticing my attention had drifted.

"I'm thinking you can do whatever you set your mind to."

She rested her chin in her palm and stared across the table at me. "Why do I get the feeling that was meant to be dirty?"

I laughed. "Probably because it took everything in me not to follow it up with 'or you could just do me and all would be right in the world.'"

She shook her head in amusement as her eyes shifted around the quiet restaurant. "I knew it had to be something like that."

I reached across the table and linked my hand with hers. Hers was so delicate and soft. The exact opposite of my massive hands made to catch fifty-yard bombs from my QB Caden. "I like that you know me. I don't let many people get close to me."

She tilted her head, her eyes focused on mine. "Why's that?"

I shrugged. "Just not something I do."

"Is that what all your one liners are about?"

I laughed. "No, those are because I'm funny and can pull off charming like no one's business."

"My psych degree would argue it's your way of keeping people from digging deeper."

I couldn't hide the amusement in my eyes. "Oh, so you think I'm trying to distract people with my charm?"

"Just saying."

I sipped the remains of my water wondering if she was on to something.

"Well, I appreciate you letting me in," Marin said.

My voice lowered. "It's you who let me in."

She rolled her eyes. "I left that one wide open for you, huh?"

"Yep." I laughed, loving our easy banter. "I was serious, you know?"

"About what?"

"When I said you've surpassed my wildest expectations," I explained.

"You're already getting laid tonight. You don't need to work so hard."

I laughed which broadened her smile. Man, I could see a future looking at that smile.

Fuuuuuck.

I was in deep shit if I didn't get my head on straight. Football was just around the corner and there I sat thinking about a future with a woman. Had I gone and lost my mind? My professional dreams had never taken a backseat to anything or anyone. What the hell was she doing to me?

"Where'd you grow up?" I asked, trying to focus on the here and now and not the fact that I didn't know what the hell I was doing.

"Mobile. Why?"

I brushed my thumb over the back of her hand. "I just wanna know more about you."

She cocked her head. "More than what I sound like and taste like?"

"Everything," I assured her.

She snickered. "There's not much to know."

"I don't think that's true. What makes you so strong?"

She grimaced. "Strong? I'm barely keeping it together most days."

"You're allowed to feel, Marin. You've been hurt. It's not weak to cry. It's what you do after the tears. And you…" I fixed her with my eyes. "You always do what you need to do."

"Thanks," she said. "Now tell me something about *you.*"

"You mean other than what I sound like and taste like?" I teased.

She stuck out her tongue and instead of being childish, it was one of the hottest things I'd ever seen.

"I'm supposed to go top five in the draft."

Her eyes lit up with excitement. "Top five? That's amazing."

I nodded, feeling a little embarrassed to be tooting my own horn. But I'd found out recently and wanted to tell someone. Being with Marin made me eager to tell her and see her reaction. Eager to see her pride in me.

"You must be really good."

I tilted my head. The look I gave her should've been answer enough, but I couldn't resist. "Look at me. Of course I am."

She rolled her eyes as she shook her head. "When's the draft?"

"April."

She squeezed my hand gently. "Well, I hope it happens for you."

"Thanks."

"Okay. So tell me something else."

I considered what to tell her. "Well…you know I skipped a grade. Do you know why?"

Her lips tipped up in the corners. "You're super smart?"

"I knew enough to pursue you, didn't I?"

"Wow," she laughed. "The lines just keep on coming."

I tossed back my head in laughter, loving how everything with Marin was so easy.

"Come on. Spill it."

"Apparently, my IQ was off the charts for an eight-year-old, so my mother demanded I skip the next grade. Forget the fact that my scores were far superior to other kids my age, you don't argue with Janine Forester. If she wants her son to skip a grade, her son skips a grade."

"How was it growing up with her?" The wondrous look in Marin's eyes told me she seriously wanted to know.

"Probably as you'd expect. A lot of eye rolling behind her back and making myself scarce when she put her foot in her mouth." I laughed to myself, realizing I'd never put into words my feelings about either of my parents before. "Obviously my parents are polar opposites. My father is caring but quiet, while my mother can't keep quiet to save her life. I think the reason they stayed married for so long is because he travels so much for work. He doesn't see it on a daily basis."

"That would make it easier."

"Yeah. But don't get me wrong. It sucks having a big mouth for a mother. I can only tolerate it because she *is* my mother. And she's always loved me fiercely and completely. I assure you, no one would hurt her son and live to tell about it."

"Did you add that part for my benefit?"

I shook my head. "You'd never hurt me."

She tightened her grip on my hand, confirming what I already knew.

"I've got another question for *you*," I said, knowing there was something that had been on my mind.

"Shoot."

"Was CJ planned?"

Marin's head shot back. "What?"

"Did you and the douchebag discuss having kids or did it just happen?"

She pulled in a deep breath and let it out slowly. "Wow. Going right for the deep stuff, huh?"

"Sorry. Is that not all right to ask?"

She did one of those shrug-nods. "It's fine…" Her gaze wandered toward the waiter who passed by our table. "I remember taking the test and finding out I was pregnant. I was so excited, but the thought of telling Charles scared me. For some reason, I didn't think he'd be as happy as I was."

"Was he?"

She shrugged as her eyes slid back to mine. "He never said he wasn't. But he also didn't get all excited like I did. I assumed that was a guy's reaction, but now I realize there's only one reaction."

"Unless you're a douchebag."

A dry laugh escaped her. "Hindsight."

"I've got another question," I said.

"Should I brace myself?"

"Nah. I just wanna know what it'll take to be part of your universe."

I watched nervousness fill her eyes. "What?"

"I want to be part of what you and CJ have, Marin."

She tilted her head thoughtfully. "You already are."

I shook my head. "That's not what I meant."

"Trace," she sighed. "You're leaving."

"Fuck that. I'll be three hours away."

Her mouth twisted, her eyes searching the room for who knows what. "We're just having fun."

"That's the point. I want to continue having fun."

Her mouth parted then closed, like she didn't know what to say.

Damn straight she didn't.

I pulled out enough cash to cover the check and tossed it down on the table. Then leaned across the table and lowered my voice. "I think you're forgetting just how much fun we have together. But don't worry. I'm up for reminding you." Given the fearful look in her eyes as I stood and grabbed her hand, she was both afraid and turned on. "When I'm back at school, I want you to remember every second we were together."

Her cheeks flushed as I pulled her to her feet. In her hot heels, she was almost my height. We walked out of the restaurant and stepped onto the sidewalk. It was a gorgeous night and the tiny white lights in the trees lining the street made it appear as if it had been staged for our first date.

"Thank you for dinner," she said.

"You don't have to—"

"Marin?" a woman called.

Both our heads twisted over our shoulders.

An older couple strolled toward us. Marin tried to drop my hand which only made me hold on tighter. The woman's gaze took us in, appraising us with curious eyes before focusing on our conjoined hands. "I thought that was you," the woman said, her eyes lifting to Marin's.

"Hi, Susan." Marin smiled warmly, her gaze shifting to the man. "James."

James looked to me, studying me with narrowed eyes.

I reached out my free hand. "Trace Forester."

"Bama's wide receiver?"

"The one and only," I assured him as he eagerly shook my hand.

Susan's eyes lit up as she drank me in. "You're even bigger in person."

"That's what Marin said, too," I said, unable to contain my grin as Marin's mouth dropped open.

"I was going to ask how you and your son were doing," Susan said to Marin. "But it looks like you're doing just fine."

"Oh, she definitely is," I answered for her.

Marin's cheeks flushed, and I had a feeling she wanted to haul off and whack me.

"Well, it was nice to see you both," Marin said, her hand squeezing mine in a death grip.

"Yeah, nice to meet you," I added, my eyes jumping between them. "Gotta get my date home."

"Good night," Marin said, as she pulled me away. Once they were out of earshot, I burst out laughing. Marin shoved me. "You have no boundaries, do you?"

"I thought that's what you like about me?"

"James is one of the partners at Charles' law firm."

"So?"

Marin sighed. "So, it's only a matter of time before Charles finds out."

"Finds out what?" I stopped at my truck parked on the side of the street, wanting nothing more than for Marin to articulate what was going on between us.

She cocked her head, remaining tight-lipped.

I backed her into the passenger door and braced my hands on the window on either side of her head. "Who cares if he finds out?"

"I don't want to add any fuel to Charles' fire. I can't lose CJ."

"I dare him to try anything."

She stared into my eyes, hers narrowing in contemplation. "Why is it I believe you?"

"Because with me, you always get the truth." I leaned in and covered her mouth with mine, loving the way she always relaxed into me, like it was the only place she truly felt safe.

Marin

Pounding on the front door sent Trace and me shooting up from my bed. Disoriented, my eyes flashed around the dark room. My alarm clock read two in the morning. I grabbed Trace's shirt that was strewn across the bedside lamp and pulled it over my head. I jumped out of bed, leaving him to grab his boxers from the floor and pull them on.

The pounding intensified.

"Wait, Marin. Let me." Trace rushed by me, down the stairs, and to the front door.

"Marin, open the fucking door!" Charles yelled from outside.

Trace's eyes flared as he yanked open the door and stepped onto the steps, unconcerned that he only wore boxers. I moved into the doorway behind him, his shirt I'd thrown on hanging down to my thighs.

"What the fuck is this?" Charles' face contorted as his eyes jumped between us.

"What's it matter to you?" Trace challenged.

"This is my house."

"Where's CJ, Charles?" I asked.

"With my parents," he spat, stepping closer toward us, his hazy gaze and abrasiveness an indicator he'd been drinking.

"Dude, you're gonna need to take a step back."

"*Dude?*" Charles' eyes jumped to me. "You're fucking a God damned kid, Marin. Is that what it's come to?"

Trace cracked his neck from side to side, apparently ready to take Charles out. "I'm gonna say it again. You're gonna need to step the fuck back and stop speaking to her like that. Better yet, don't speak to her at all."

"Did you talk to James?" I asked him.

Charles' face scrunched. "James?"

"Isn't that why you're here?"

"I'm here because this is my fucking house. And you're my fucking wife."

Trace stepped forward.

Knowing he could've leveled Charles with a single blow, I moved to him, grabbing onto his arm to let him know it's not what I wanted. At least at that moment. Four months ago at the Mercury Hotel would've been a different story.

That's when it hit me.

That's when it all made sense.

"Did she break up with you?" I asked Charles.

Charles' eyes shot away.

Son of a bitch.

"The papers have been filed, Charles. Whether you're with her or not, we're over."

He lifted his chin toward Trace. "Because of him?"

A disapproving laugh shot out of me. "Because of you. Because of what you did. I know what I deserve now. Somewhere along the way I think I forgot."

Despite a drunken Charles standing there, Trace wrapped his arm around me and pulled me into him, dropping a kiss to the crown of my head.

"Don't forget who pays this mortgage," Charles warned. "I can have the police here in five minutes."

"For what, Charles? What have I done wrong?" I asked.

He stared back at me, his blank gaze a stark reminder of the emptiness behind his eyes and the unhappiness I felt with him in my life.

"If you want the house, take it up with the lawyers. Then, once everything's official, CJ and I will leave. For now, go home. Be at your parents' when CJ wakes up and spend time with him. He deserves that."

"Come on," Trace said.

I nodded as he turned me into the house and closed the door behind us.

Trace pulled me into a hug and stared down at me. "You did good out there."

"I meant what I said. I know what I deserve."

Trace's lips slipped into a cocky grin. "Damn straight you do."

Distracting me from the sound of Charles' car peeling out of the driveway, Trace captured my lips, before lifting me off my feet and carrying me upstairs.

CHAPTER THIRTEEN
AUGUST

Marin

From the spot on my blanket at the far end of the beach, I watched surfers trying to catch a wave. Sunbathers absorbing the mid-afternoon sun. The volleyball players diving into the sand making save after save. It was a picturesque day, and all I wanted to do was take it all in. Soon, CJ would be starting in school, Trace would be back on campus, and I'd be busy with my own school and job.

"Hey, Mom," CJ called as he ran toward me soaked, his legs covered in the sand he kicked up. Much to my relief, he'd returned a week after Charles' late night visit. And he was still the same amazing kid, unchanged by his prick of a father.

"Have fun?" I asked.

"Yeah," CJ said as he dropped to the sand a few feet in front of my blanket and began digging with the shovel and sifter he'd left there earlier.

Trace approached, having walked up from the water instead of ran. And though he was just as soaked as CJ and his feet were covered with sand, it was his body that had every woman and girl in a fifty-foot radius following his strides back to our blanket.

I wasn't blind. I noticed the looks he received everywhere we went, but I ignored it because he did. The great thing about him was whenever we were together, his attention was always focused solely on me.

Trace sat down beside me on the blanket, quickly dropping a wet kiss on my lips while CJ was preoccupied. He was always good about not doing anything that would be awkward for CJ. "That was so much fun," he said.

"What was?" I asked, the salt from his lips lingering on mine.

"Just playing in the water. I haven't done that in a long time?"

I tipped my head. "You let me go in alone last time we were here," I said. "Could've been a lot of fun if you'd come in."

He groaned. "Believe me. It took everything in me that night not to come in after you."

"Maybe we can try that again before you leave."

His brows lifted. "Is that a promise?"

I shrugged. "Unless you plan on wussing out again,"

He threw back his head and laughed. Then he shook out his wet hair, sending water droplets flying all over me.

I rolled onto my side away from him in laughter.

"You still wanna call me a wuss?" he asked.

I glanced over my shoulder, looking him dead in the eyes. "Wuss."

His eyes flared. "I assure you, if we end up here again, there's no chance I'm wussing out."

"I'll believe it when I see it," I teased.

He grinned, standing and moving toward CJ. "Now, if you'll excuse me, I need to teach my man the proper way to build a sand castle."

I spent the rest of the day watching the two of them construct a lopsided sand castle. Anyone walking by wouldn't have known what it was, but CJ was so proud of that castle. He asked me to take pictures of him and Trace in front of it so he could show my parents. And God love him, Trace acted like it was the best thing he'd ever seen.

Trace

"Madison, Wisconsin and…Cheyenne, Wyoming," CJ said from the backseat of my truck.

"Buddy, you got them all right." I glanced at him in the rearview mirror. "I'm so proud of you."

"I've been practicing with Mom," he boasted.

"That is so cool."

CJ and I had spent the morning fishing. We hadn't caught anything, but it didn't matter. We had a great time talking and enjoying the time together. I pulled into his driveway beside Marin's car and threw it into park.

"Are you Mom's boyfriend?" CJ asked.

I killed the engine and turned to look at him. "Would that be a bad thing?"

He shook his head. "No. But the way my dad said it, it sounded bad and I didn't like it."

I threw open my door and marched around to CJ's side. I didn't think it was possible to hate someone more than I hated his father. I opened his door and unbuckled him. "Well, I'm a boy. And your mom's my friend. So, I guess your dad had it right."

"Would it be okay if I didn't call you *my* boyfriend?" he asked as I helped him down from the truck.

I grabbed his fishing pole from the floor of the backseat and laughed. "Yeah, buddy. No need."

"Good," he said with a smile as he took the pole from me. "Because you're not my boyfriend. You're my best friend."

My heart constricted. The kid had a direct line to it. And with each passing day, his presence in my life—and my need for him and Marin in it—was becoming more and more solidified. It just sucked that by evening, I'd be back on campus and two hundred miles away from them. "I think that sounds perfect."

"Hey," Marin said.

My eyes shot to the front steps. *Holy hell.* All I could see were her long legs in her hot little cutoffs. My eyes traveled up and over her tight T-shirt. She'd undoubtedly worn the outfit to remind me of what I'd be leaving behind. "Hey." I gave her one more purposeful once over, drinking her in since I had no idea when I'd see her in person again for a while.

As I moved toward her, her eyes shifted to the boxes and crates filling the bed of my truck. Sadness swept over her features before she plastered on the fakest smile I'd ever seen. She ticked her head toward her house. "Mind coming inside?"

"Not at all." How the hell was I gonna get by without these two?

Once we stepped inside, Marin asked CJ to give us a couple minutes. Without the slightest fuss, he took off upstairs. "Sit," she said, gesturing toward the sofa.

I cocked my head. "Everything okay?"

She nodded, but her eyes said otherwise.

I dropped onto the sofa, surprising her by pulling her down onto my lap. She yelped as I buried my lips in her neck and assaulted her with open-mouthed kisses that made her purr. She somehow extricated my lips and swiveled to face me. She cupped my cheeks between her palms, making sure she had my undivided attention. "While you're gone, I'll be right here." Her words were slow and deliberate. "I'm not going anywhere."

I laughed. "I know that."

She shook her head, her eyes serious. "Go to school, play football, and get your degree. I have all the time in the world."

Her words took me aback. "I plan to."

"Good. Then just promise me you'll have fun."

I scoffed. "You might need to define 'fun.'"

She smiled. "Within reason." Her lightheartedness quickly disappeared and her eyes became focused and serious again. "And if for some reason you find someone who does it for you more than me—"

My lips stole the rest of her words. Her ridiculous yet vulnerable words. Was that what this was about? Was she worried I'd fuck around? Was she worried I'd abandon her too? When I pulled back, she was breathless and dazed, just the way I wanted her. My words were just as slow and deliberate as hers. "*You* do it for me."

She tilted her head. "I just wanted it said."

"Well, you said it."

Her eyes drifted from mine as her hands slipped from my cheeks.

"Hey. Look at me."

She did.

"We're gonna be okay. I want you and CJ in my life. No distance is gonna change that."

She forced a smile.

The true scope of what I was doing by leaving lay in her eyes and unspoken words. I was making her question everything between us. I was making her worry I wouldn't return. I was making her fear I wouldn't be faithful. "Have I ever given you a reason not to trust me?"

She shook her head.

"Then how can I make it clear I'll be back?"

Her lips twisted as she shrugged. "Just come back."

I nodded. "Deal."

"And give me your shirt."

My nose wrinkled. "What shirt?"

She pinched the front of the plain white T-shirt I wore. "This one."

I grinned. "Why?"

"Because I want to sleep in it," she said matter-of-factly.

Without a word, I reached behind my head and tugged the shirt off, handing it to her.

She snatched it from me and brought it to her nose. "Oh, good. It smells like you."

I leaned in and kissed her, hoping to alleviate her fears. "I'll call you tonight. How do you feel about phone sex?"

She laughed. "Never tried it."

My lips slipped into a cocky grin. "Oh, we're gonna have some fun."

She laughed before I kissed her again, wanting to leave her with absolutely no doubt that I'd be back for her soon.

CHAPTER FOURTEEN

Trace

"I barely heard from you this summer," Caden said.

I glanced to him sitting beside me at the bar at our favorite off-campus hangout—the only one that took my fake ID. The team returned weeks before classes began, so the bar was dead. And given the flood of females who usually showed up, especially once word got out my quarterback roommate and I were there, it was great to have the place to ourselves. "I was busy," I said, lifting my bottle of beer to my mouth. Once the season started, I kept my drinking to a minimum. But since it was Friday night *and* the first time all week Caden and I weren't exhausted after a grueling practice in the hundred-degree heat, I was indulging.

"You make a lot of cash at the beach?" Caden asked, his eyes on the television watching preseason college football analysis and spotlights.

"The usual."

Caden's phone vibrated on the bar. His girlfriend Finlay's name lit up the screen.

My eyes moved back to the television as he answered the call. A clip of one of my catches from last season filled the screen. I watched it, mesmerized by my own skills.

When I was out on the field, it all came naturally. Running. Catching. Being in the right spot on the field to make the big catch. I loved football. I breathed football. I could see myself doing it for a very long time. It's why at the end of the season, I planned to declare myself eligible for the draft. I could've gone this year, but in my heart, I knew I needed college under my belt. And just like Caden who'd stuck around for his senior year, I wanted to continue playing for an outstanding coach while improving my stats and breaking a few more records. Then, after I'd accomplished all that, I'd go pro.

"I fucking loved that play," Caden said as he hung up with Finlay and caught the tail end of my catch.

I shrugged. "I'm awesome. What can I say?"

"You do realize I threw you that ball?"

I loved busting Caden's balls. "You were there?"

He shoved me, practically knocking me off my stool. "Fuck you."

We laughed before settling in and watching some of the opponents we'd face during the season get their spotlights. There'd be some stiff competition, but we had a great team—if our offensive line got their asses in shape. They always started the season slow. And this season would make it or break it for me. A losing team didn't get the same attention the better teams got. And if our offensive line sucked and Caden couldn't get me the ball, I could kiss the pros goodbye.

* * *

"I missed you tonight," I said.

Marin's face filled the screen on my phone. It had been a week since I'd seen her in person. We talked every day, but it wasn't the same as actually being there. "Oh yeah?" Her voice was raspy, her eyes sleepy as she too lay in bed.

I'd woken her up, but now that I had her on the phone there was no way in hell I was hanging up. "That's where you were supposed to say you missed me and all my hotness too."

She laughed. "Of course I miss you."

"That's better."

"So, have there been any girls trying to move in on my man?" she asked.

"Your man? I like the sound of that."

"Is that you avoiding my question?"

I laughed. "Fine. I had to beat them off with a stick. There were definite tears shed, but I escaped unscathed."

She laughed.

Damn, I missed that laugh.

"I have something for you," she said.

I lifted my brows. "Oh, yeah?"

She nodded, a devilish twinkle in her eyes. "Are you watching?"

"Watching what?"

She moved the phone away from her face, pulling it back so I could see she was wearing a tight-as-sin Alabama T-shirt torn near her cleavage—revealing way more than I'd ever let any other guy see.

I could feel myself getting hard. I usually took care of business after we spoke. But maybe she'd be up for some fun tonight.

"Do you like?" she asked, moving the phone back so I could see her face.

"Are you kidding? You look hot."

She laughed. "Well, that's not all."

"There's more?"

She nodded. "Hold on." She'd clearly gotten up. The screen bounced all around her room. When it came into focus, she was standing in front of her bedroom mirror holding the phone so I could see her back. *Sweet-baby-Jesus.* My last name and number were on the back of the shirt. And her ass looked damn good in my favorite red thong. She knew just what to do to get me all hot and bothered when I was almost two hundred miles away from her.

"Now would be a good time for that phone sex," I said.

Her sleepy laugh carried through the phone before she lay back down on her bed with her face filling the screen. "So, you like your surprise?"

"Like it? I love it."

"I had it made. I thought they'd sell them, but I guess that's against university policy or something to make money off you guys."

"That or they wouldn't be able to keep my number in stock."

She laughed again and all I wanted to do was wrap my arms around her and hold her.

Okay, so maybe I wanted to fuck her silly then hold her. Regardless, what it boiled down to was me wanting her. In every way possible. And that notion scared the fuck out of me.

I was nineteen. I was in my prime. I could have any girl I wanted. But the one I wanted was three hours away with a kid and a soon-to-be ex-husband. Strange how things happened. But it had happened. And I considered myself one lucky son of a bitch. So, I was gonna do everything in my power not to screw it up. "You do realize you're not wearing that to my games," I informed her.

"Why? I think it makes my boobs look great."

"That's exactly why you're not wearing it," I growled.

She laughed. "I'm joking. It's for your eyes only."

"Damn straight, woman."

She rolled onto her side with her cheek resting on her pillow and her eyelids drooping with sleep as she stared at me. "Did you have fun tonight?"

I rolled onto my side, wanting to feel like I was there with her, at least for a little while. "It was fun hanging out with Caden again."

"After hanging out with a five-year-old all summer, you were probably starved for guy talk."

"You know I loved every second of that."

She nodded. "So, did he."

"Is he getting excited for school to start?"

"Yeah. I bought him a backpack. You've gotta see how cute he looks with it on. The thing's almost as big as he is."

I laughed, imagining him on his first day, all excited but nervous.

"You tired?" she asked.

"Yeah. Football's been kicking my ass this week. I'm not in as good of shape as I thought I was."

"My body would beg to differ."

I smiled, loving how she could work those comments in as well as I could. Guess I *was* rubbing off on her.

"I'm sure it'll get easier. Because, from what you tell me, you're pretty amazing on the field."

I feigned surprise. "I told you that?"

Her sleepy laughter carried through the phone, filling my otherwise empty room with the much-needed sound. "Only a hundred times."

I snickered. "I'm also amazing in the bedroom."

"Yeah," she sighed. "That's why it's a shame you're not here."

"I don't need to be there to make you moan."

Her breath hitched and her eyes widened.

"Lay on your back," I said as blood rushed to my balls.

Marin gnawed on her bottom lip, contemplating my words for all of two seconds before she held the phone above her so I could see her face as she did as told. "Okay."

My voice lowered. "Now take your hand and slide it down your stomach so I can see."

She tilted the phone so I could see her hand glide over her stomach and down to the waistband of her thong.

"Now slip your hand inside."

Her hand crept slowly under the band until I knew her fingertips were right where we both wanted them.

"Don't move them."

She gasped. "Why not?"

"Because I said so."

She snickered.

"Now, I want you to use your finger and glide it around as you picture me there with you. Picture my face between your legs and my mouth on you."

I watched her finger moving under the almost-see-through material of her thong, and instantly I was hard as a rock.

"That's my tongue, Marin. Around and around until the throbbing becomes too much. Until I know your body is aching for me to do more. And then, when you think I'm about to ease that ache, I breathe you in. Because your scent destroys me every fucking time."

Marin whimpered.

"Now I want you to add another finger and push them both inside."

Her breath rushed out of her. "I can't hold the phone anymore."

I smirked, loving that I could affect her regardless of the distance between us. "Put it beside you."

She did and I was granted a prime view of her ceiling.

"Are you pushing them in and out?" I asked, though her heavy breathing filling the silence told me she was.

"God, yes."

"Tell me how it feels?"

"Not as good as you," she said, all raspy and hot. "You're so much bigger."

"Damn straight I am, baby," I laughed.

A cross between a laugh and her breath rushed out of her.

"And you like me inside you?"

"*Yessss.*"

"You're close, aren't you?"

Her soft purr told me she was.

"I want you to move your fingers back to your clit. Circle it like my tongue would. Around and around and around."

"Oh, God."

"Keep going, Marin. Feel my mouth. I'm just about to suck on it and make you see stars."

And just like that, she moaned my name. Her shaky breaths dragged in and out of her.

And even though I was hard as a fucking boulder and alone in my room, I couldn't believe how satisfied I felt to be able to bring her such pleasure.

Marin eventually picked up her phone and her flushed cheeks filled my screen. "Wow."

I laughed. "I promised we'd keep having fun. And I always deliver."

She smiled, but her heavy eyelids told me she needed to sleep.

"Thank you," I said, wishing I was there with her.

She cocked her head, confused by my words. "I should be thanking you."

"Oh, you will as soon as I see you again," I laughed. "But I meant thanks for being so amazing."

She blinked a long drawn out blink. "Right back at ya, Forester."

CHAPTER FIFTEEN

Marin

Damn Charles. Even though he promised CJ he'd be there, I knew he wouldn't show up. I just knew it.

I scanned the large crowd gathered outside CJ's school. Eager parents snapped pictures of their kids while CJ and I snapped a couple selfies before I had him pose for a few shots alone.

A teacher stepped out of the main door and the crowd quieted. "We're going to start with kindergarten. Once your name is called, please move to the side of the building and form a line."

My heart began to race. This was it. This was the day my little boy began school. His first step to becoming whatever it was he wanted to be in life. The whole idea was bittersweet for me. It was the start of a new chapter in his life. And in mine. I began school the following week and a part time job in the psychology department doing clerical work.

I gripped CJ's hand and straightened my shoulders, trying to be strong.

A hand slipped into my free hand. My head shot to my right, completely expecting it to be Charles. My breath caught in my throat as Trace leaned in and planted a quick kiss on my lips, stunning me still.

He moved over to CJ whose face lit up as he squatted down in front of him and placed his hands on his shoulders, looking him right in the eyes and uttering words I couldn't hear. Whatever they were, they brought a huge smile to CJ's face.

Tears glazed my eyes as Trace stood and dropped his arm around my shoulders.

He'd shown up. Right when I needed him most, he'd shown up.

The teacher continued rattling off her list of names. She finally called CJ. He turned and wrapped his arms around me, his small arms holding on tightly. Then he released me and moved to Trace, doing the same. I swiped away at the corners of my eyes to stop the tears from falling as I watched CJ waddle off with his enormous backpack.

Trace pulled me into his side. I went willingly, wrapping my arms around his waist. I needed his strength more than I realized. "You did good," he whispered before dropping a kiss on the top of my head.

"I can't believe you came."

"I wouldn't miss his big day for anything."

I pulled back and looked up at him. "But what about practice?"

"It's not until five." He dropped his forehead to mine. "And if you haven't figured it out by now, I want to be here for you and CJ."

We both turned just in time to see CJ and his classmates follow the teacher into the building, disappearing from view. I released a long breath. My little boy was gone. And Trace had shown up to be my rock. I hadn't asked him to. He just knew what I needed. "I've missed you."

He quirked his brow. "How much?"

I tilted my head. I hadn't seen him in over two weeks, so my eyes absorbed his features. God, I'd missed his eyes. His dimples. His cocky smirk. "Do you have to head back right now?"

His eyes actually twinkled. "I could be persuaded to stay a little while longer."

I laughed as he led me away from the crowd and toward the parking lot, determined to get me alone.

From what he told me later that night, he made it back just in time for practice.

CHAPTER SIXTEEN
SEPTEMBER

Marin

I rushed out of the building where I worked. It was still hot as hell in Alabama, so the pants and blouse I wore to work stuck to my skin as I hurried across campus toward my Group Counseling class. My phone rang in my pocket. I slipped it out and my cousin Jerry's name filled the screen. Since CJ returned from his father's last month, I hadn't spoken to Jerry which gave me hope that Charles realized it was hard work being a single parent. I lifted the phone to my ear. "Hi, Jerry."

"Hey. Sorry I haven't been in touch. But things have been at a standstill until now."

"Until now? What does that mean?"

"Charles wants you to call off the divorce."

A huge belly laugh burst out of me. I needed to stop at the nearest bench to sit and control my laughter. "That's hysterical. Does he want us to renew our vows too?"

"He's serious," Jerry said, his grim tone stopping my laughter. "He's contesting the divorce."

I stilled. "What does that even mean?"

"It means you can move forward with the divorce, but it'll take time and money to respond to the petition, and gather subpoenas and depositions. I'm not gonna lie. It's stressful and will end with a judge and a hearing."

I sat there staring out at the blur of students passing by. What I wouldn't have given to be an undergrad again. To have no worries. No responsibilities. No ex who won't disappear. "He can do whatever he wants," I told Jerry. "Just make it clear I'm not calling off the divorce."

"He seems ready to drag it out," Jerry warned.

"Then let him. It's still over."

Trace

Caden and I walked into the bookstore with the list of books we needed for our classes. Gauging by the line wrapped around the store, most of the school had returned to campus and headed straight there.

Heads turned as we made our way down the first aisle, passing the anatomy, anthropology, and astronomy books neither of us needed for our majors. We were used to the attention we received. All the stares when we entered a room. All the whispers when we passed by.

Grady, our annoying as hell right tackle, appeared out of nowhere and squeezed between us, throwing his arms around our shoulders. "Have you seen all the fresh meat in here?"

Caden and I made fast work of ducking out from his arms.

"Caden's taken, dude," I said, trying to distance myself from him. "And Finlay would kick your ass if she heard you talking like that with him."

Grady grimaced. He and Finlay, who was not just Caden's girlfriend but also the team's water girl, had gotten off on the wrong foot last year. And she was the only one I ever saw put the three-hundred-pounder in his place.

"And what about you, Grady?" Caden asked him. "Thought you and Yvette had a thing going?"

"Yeah, well, she found some statistics geek she said she has more in common with."

"No way?" I pretended to be surprised.

Grady shrugged. "Ah well, that just leaves me available for all the hot freshmen who need an older guy to show them the ropes."

"More like the way to the dining hall," I said as Caden burst out laughing.

Grady's attention quickly moved to a cute little redhead that walked by. He abruptly ditched us to follow her in the opposite direction.

"He can be such a douche," I said.

"Ah." Caden pulled a book off the shelf and checked the price on the back. "He's not all bad."

"Hey, Forester."

I glanced to my right. A girl I'd hooked up with last year stood beside me in her shorter-than-short cutoffs that would undoubtedly reveal her ass cheeks once she walked away. "Hey."

"Tara," she offered.

"I knew that," I lied.

She shot me a knowing grin, probably because not only did she know it was a lie, but she also knew what I looked like naked. "We should hang out again some time," she said.

"Oh…yeah." I fumbled for the words. I hadn't considered how to maneuver when it came to all the willing females I'd be around. Did I make it known I was in a relationship, or just keep myself out of awkward situations? I'd never had a girlfriend before. These were uncharted waters for me. "I've got your number," I assured her, like that said it all.

"Yeah. I hope you use it."

I smiled, feeling like a complete douche. I wasn't purposely letting on that I was single, but I didn't come right out and tell her it ain't happening either. Was I not ready to be committed to only one girl? Was I purposely sabotaging what Marin and I had? Were my feelings not as strong as I thought they were?

"See you around," Tara said, walking away so I could get a clear shot of her ass cheeks.

Caden shook his head. "The Forester charm never ceases to amaze me. I'll meet you at the registers."

"All right." I turned to the shelf beside me and scanned the titles for the book I needed for biochemistry. Thanks to the guilty knot twisting in my gut, I suddenly couldn't focus. I had a good thing going with Marin. But I hadn't considered what it would be like to be back on campus. In the past, it was a free-for-all. I had no one holding me back. Is that what Marin meant when she sat me down? Did she realize what school would be like for me? All the girls? All the temptation? Was she already braced for the end?

I liked to believe I was a stand-up guy, but would keeping it in my pants be more difficult than I initially thought? I wasn't some manwhore. I didn't need sex every night. Well, maybe I did, but I could control the urge because I wanted this thing with Marin to work. It had been so easy at home. But would the distance destroy us? I'd worked so hard to get her to want to be with me. I'd be no better than her ex if I wasn't strong enough for her. For us.

Once I found my biochemistry book, I headed three aisles over to find my sports medicine book. My phone vibrated in my pocket. I pulled it out, smiling when I saw CJ's name on my screen. I lifted it to my ear. "What's up, buddy?"

"Hi, Trace. I won my flag football game today."

"Buddy, that's awesome." I still couldn't get over the fact that he'd signed up for football because he wanted to be like me.

"Yeah. I almost had a touchdown but some big kid pulled my flag on the five-yard line."

"That's okay. You've got plenty of time to score touchdowns."

"That's what Mom said."

I couldn't wipe the grin off my face. "I'm so proud of you."

"That's what Mom said, too."

I laughed to myself. It was killing me to miss his games. I wanted to be there for him. Wanted to be there for Marin. It had been two weeks since his first day of school. Since I'd seen them in person. And every day was getting more and more difficult.

Caden rounded the corner and stared at me with furrowed brows. What had he heard?

"Well, I just wanted to tell you the good news," CJ said.

"Okay. Thanks." I wanted to ask to talk to Marin, but the way Caden was watching me, I didn't want to open myself up to questions. I had a big mouth for a mother. I kept my personal shit to myself. Good or bad, it was mine to tell.

Marin

Trace ran down the field in Tennessee on Saturday afternoon, nabbing an amazing pass over his head on the thirty-yard line. CJ and I leapt off the sofa screaming and jumping up and down as Trace ran with a group of opponents on his tail past the twenty-five-yard line…the twenty…the fifteen…the ten…the five…and right into the end zone.

Even though they were in enemy territory in Tennessee, the crowd still erupted. Trace spiked the ball into the end zone as his teammates jumped all over him.

I stood there staring at him on television. I was so incredibly proud of him. Not to mention hot and bothered. I'd seen him naked. I'd touched him in every place imaginable. I'd had him inside me. Now he was this larger-than-life superstar on television elating the entire state of Alabama.

My attention moved to CJ who danced around the living room with his hands in the air shaking his little butt around. It was adorable. I recorded him and sent it off to Trace so he'd see it as soon as he returned to the locker room. I dropped down onto the sofa, so eager for the offense to be back on the field so I could see him again.

A couple hours later, I was snuggled on the sofa having already put CJ to bed when Trace's name appeared on my phone. Those same anxious butterflies I got every time he called fluttered wildly. I tried to be quiet but I couldn't contain my excitement as I answered the phone. "Hi."

"So, what'd you think?" he asked.

"You were *amazing*."

He laughed. "See? What have I been telling you?"

I chuckled at his unyielding ego. "Did you get the video?"

"Yeah. It was awesome."

"He was so proud of you," I assured him.

"He the only one?"

I rolled my eyes at my empty room. "No."

His voice lowered to the same deep tenor he used when we were in bed. "Did it turn you on?"

Shivers rushed up my legs as visions of him in those tight pants and body-hugging shirt that gripped his biceps flooded my brain. "And then some."

There was background noise on his end and then silence. Was someone there? His roommate? A girl? "Can I call you later?" he whispered.

The sudden halt to our conversation filled me with nervousness. "Yeah. Of course."

"Okay."

"Okay," I echoed.

When he disconnected the call, an uneasy pit formed in my stomach. He'd called as soon as he could which meant he was thinking of me, so why the quick brush off? Who was there with him? Why couldn't he talk in front of them? I'd never considered Trace would cheat on me. But then again, I'd never expected Charles would either.

It had been so much easier when Trace and I could see each other. And sleep next to each other. And love each other.

Love?

Shit.

Trace

"Who were you talking to?" Caden asked as he stepped out of the bathroom. The steam from his second shower of the night billowed out into our hotel room.

I tucked my phone into my pocket and got comfortable on my bed. "A friend."

"Same friend you were talking to in the bookstore the other day?"

"Fuck off."

"Don't worry. I'm hitting the gym later so you can call whoever it was back."

"Is that what you and Finlay are calling it this year?" I asked.

"Dude, we really were in the gym last year."

"I thought it was the pool?" I said, trying to push his buttons.

"Fine. And the pool."

"Actually…it's not *where* you were I'm doubting. It's what you were doing."

He laughed.

Truth be told. I was only busting his balls out of jealousy. His girlfriend traveled with the team. He got to see her whenever he wanted. I didn't have that luxury and it was beginning to suck.

When Caden left a couple hours later, I slipped out my phone. It was late, but I promised to call Marin back, so I wanted to at least text her. My thumbs went to work on the screen. **I need to see you again.**

It took a minute, but the dots indicating she was typing popped up. **I need to see you again too.**

I smiled, practically hearing her raspy voice. **I'll try to come home soon.**

I'll be here.

CHAPTER SEVENTEEN

Marin

I tucked my laptop into my bag at the end of my career counseling class on Friday, waiting as the professor walked around the classroom returning our first test. I felt confident. My essay covered all the main points and my answers for the multiple choice and short answers came easily. Maybe the juggling act I'd been pulling off wouldn't be as difficult as I thought it would be.

When he placed the test down on my desk, my heart dropped. I checked the name to be sure it belonged to me because the number scrolled across the top in red ink, the one that looked a whole lot like a sixty-five, could *not* be mine.

Dammit.

I'd studied for the test for hours, neglecting CJ and things around the house. I'd been up all night. Reviewing my notes. Quizzing myself. What the hell had happened?

My attention lifted to my professor's disappointed eyes. I wanted to tell him no one was more disappointed than me. But why bother? I clearly wasn't cut out for the graduate program. The time off had hurt me—in more ways than one.

I ripped the test off the desk and threw my bag over my shoulder, dashing out of the classroom before I broke down in front of my classmates.

When I got to my car, I threw my bag in the backseat, not caring that half the contents rolled out onto the floor. I still needed to get home to begin writing an essay for my group counseling class that was due on Monday. But how the hell was I going to research and write on a topic when I felt so inadequate? Not to mention CJ had football practice and a game, and I needed to go grocery shopping, clean the house, and do laundry.

I buried my face in my hands. *"Shiiiit."*

After pulling it together, I picked up CJ from school and threw some waffles in the toaster. Breakfast for dinner was going to have to do. I hurried to the laundry room and dug through the clothes in the dryer that I hadn't had time to fold, pulling out his practice uniform.

I sat in the stands at his practice, highlighting portions of chapter five in my book and making notes in the margins, hoping once I got home and CJ was tucked in bed, I could gather enough information to write my essay. Juggling school, work, CJ, his activities, a long-distance relationship, and an asshole ex was getting more and more difficult.

Something had to give.

My phone vibrated on the bleacher beside me. I picked it up and found a text from Jerry. **Need you to come by my office tomorrow at noon.**

* * *

My foot bounced as I sat in Jerry's small Main Street office. His law degrees hung in mismatched frames on the wall behind his head. "You made it clear I wasn't calling off the divorce, right?"

"Yes, they know."

"Well, then what's going on? I'm barely asking for anything. And *he's* the one who cheated."

"His infidelity has already been established," Jerry said, pulling off his reading glasses and placing them down on the stack of papers on his desk. "I'm sorry to do this to you, Marin."

"Do what?" I asked.

"His legal team is questioning if there was infidelity on *your* part."

My eyes flared. "Like hell there was."

"They're saying they have proof."

"What proof? Trace and I started dating this summer. Charles and I had already been separated for months with absolutely no possibility of reconciliation."

Jerry shrugged. "His lawyers say they have proof and if we don't agree to their terms, they're going to the media."

The lines in my forehead deepened. "The media?"

"I assume Charles thinks it'll tarnish Trace's reputation. You know, dating a married woman and all."

My mouth hung open. "He wouldn't."

"I'm afraid they've drawn up his demands."

Rage flooded my body. "*His* demands?"

Jerry nodded. "I'm sorry, Marin. But since you wouldn't call off the divorce, he's ready to play dirty."

"But why? He didn't want me."

"Marin." Jerry's face softened, clearly understanding something I didn't. "You've made him look replaceable. Foolish even by dating someone younger. Better looking. A soon-to-be pro athlete. That wouldn't sit well with any man."

"Because he's jealous, he thinks he can threaten me?"

"I'm not sure his lawyers would call it threatening. They'd spin it to be in the best interest of CJ."

I shook my head. "He knows I'll never allow Trace to be hurt in this."

"That's exactly what he's banking on. He's forcing your hand."

I pulled in a deep breath. "But why? What does he want?"

"Physical custody."

It was as if the air was punched out of my lungs. "What?"

"*If* you don't break off your relationship."

My heart walloped erratically in my chest. "Can he even do that?"

"I'm afraid he can demand whatever he wants. And I'm sure he sees it as he's giving you the choice. Either you choose your son or your relationship."

I scoffed, as my eyes drifted to the only window in Jerry's office trying to hold back my tears. "He's such a thoughtful guy."

"I'm sorry, Marin," Jerry said.

"You didn't do this. He did."

* * *

I stared out the kitchen window watching CJ swing on his swing set after dinner. My eyes were puffy and my face blotchy from all the crying I'd been doing since leaving Jerry's office. I was a mess. My life was a mess. And I had absolutely no idea what I was going to do. Or how I was going to fix it.

An unexpected knock on my front door had me moving toward it. I reached the foyer and pulled it open. Trace's mother, Janine, stood on my front step. Sudden fear swept over me. "Is Trace okay?"

"He's fine," she said, giving my sweat pants and T-shirt a condescending once over. "May I come in?"

I stepped aside and she brushed by me, her eyes assessing my books strewn all over the coffee table and my opened laptop on the sofa. "Don't mind the mess. I've got an essay due Monday and a test on Tuesday." I hurried to the sofa and picked up my laptop so she could sit. "Have a seat."

She shook her head. "This won't take long."

My brows shot up. "Oh?"

"I want you to end things with Trace."

I choked on a laugh. Had she been speaking to Charles? She always did like him better than me.

"You think I'm joking?" Janine asked.

I shrugged. "I couldn't possibly know what you're thinking."

"I don't want him on campus preoccupied with you and your son. He has school and football to focus on."

"We know that."

"Don't tell me what my son knows," she spat.

I bit down on my bottom lip, stopping myself from telling her what I really thought of her.

"Do you think you're being fair to him?" she asked. "He's got his whole life ahead of him. You've lived yours."

"I'm twenty-nine."

"And he's still a kid. He doesn't need to be strapped down to a woman who's looking for a daddy for her child."

I gasped. "That's not what I'm doing. CJ has a father. An asshole, but a father nonetheless."

"Be reasonable. Trace deserves all the experiences you've already had." She began to pace, her eyes averting mine. "He deserves to make it to the pros with no regrets. He deserves to find a girl his own age. He deserves to propose and get married. He deserves to buy a house and have a child." Her eyes shot back to mine. "You've had your experiences. Your firsts. He deserves to as well."

I stood frozen to my spot. As much as I hated his mother, and hated hearing her fears, I suddenly understood them. CJ was Trace in fourteen years. What would I do if he was trying to create a future with some woman with a kid? A woman with an ex who was determined to make her life hell? Trace did deserve all those things. Starting fresh with someone his age did make sense. And for once, Janine Forester and I agreed on something.

"I can see you understand my concerns," she said, watching my internal battle play out across my face. She had no idea the real cause of my struggle. The real reason I was even considering her concerns. "Trace is blind when it comes to you and your son. He isn't seeing how ridiculous this relationship is."

Her lack of empathy toward me or my feelings felt like a knife plunging into my already battered heart.

"You're the adult. You need to end it. I know my son. He's loyal and wouldn't desert you."

Tears stung my eyes as she turned and walked out my front door without another word. Deep down I already knew what I needed to do. I didn't need her to tell me.

That night, as I lay in bed, Trace's unanswered calls and texts kept popping up on my screen. **I miss you.**
Where are you?
Call me.
Is something wrong?
Is CJ ok?

Are you ok?

I couldn't respond. Because I wasn't okay.

I needed time to think. Time to breathe. Time to consider my next move very carefully.

I had everything to lose.

Damn Charles for putting me in this situation. Damn him for forcing me to make a decision that would break two hearts. And damn Janine for giving me an excuse.

I'm coming home tomorrow night.

I gasped as Trace's next text appeared on my screen. That was too soon. I wasn't ready to face him. I needed to be sure. I needed to be certain I'd explored every possible option first. I needed to hold him off for just a little while longer. **Sorry. I won't be home.**

His text came immediately. **I'll wait.**

I switched off my phone and tossed it onto the nightstand.

Ignoring him had been a temporary fix. I knew Trace well enough to know some unanswered texts and calls wouldn't deter him—or buy me enough time for what I inevitably needed to do.

* * *

The persistent knocking on my front door the following night did not elicit the normal butterflies, but a stomach-clenching fear. I walked slowly toward the door, thankful my parents had taken CJ for the night.

I sucked in a deep breath and pulled open the door. Everything happened so fast. Trace's hands cupped my cheeks as he pinned me to the wall, slamming the door shut with his foot as his mouth covered mine. His tongue plunged inside, determinedly exploring my mouth as if starved for my taste. I didn't want to resist. I wanted to get lost in his kiss. In the feel of his body pressed against mine. In his presence in my empty house. In him. But I couldn't. I dropped my hands to his chest and pushed with every bit of strength I could muster. He didn't budge, if anything he kissed me deeper and harder.

Inevitably, he needed to catch his breath as badly as I did. He stepped back from me. Both our chests heaved as we stared across the space between us. Our need for each other practically crackled in the silence. I would've given anything to race back into his arms. To get lost in his touch.

His lips slipped into a cocky grin as his eyes drank me in. "Next time you think about ignoring me, be prepared for my wrath. Were you trying to drive me crazy?"

I shook my head.

"Well, you did."

A right hook to my face would have felt better than the way I felt seeing him in front of me looking like he missed me as much as I missed him. Like he wanted me naked and compliant. My eyes swerved away from his.

"What's wrong?"

I begrudgingly looked back to him. "Come sit down."

"I wanna take you out."

I dropped down onto the sofa, my elbows resting on my knees and my fingers wringing in front of me. "Where? Some college bar?"

His eyes narrowed from where he stood. "What?"

"Or some party where people'll think I'm someone's mother? Oh, that's right. I am."

"That doesn't happen and you know it."

"Do I?" I shook my head, tears glazing my vision. "I won't say I don't care about you, because I do."

He dropped down beside me. "Marin, what's going on?"

I stared down at my wringing hands, unable to look at him. "I can't give you what a girl your age can," I said, knowing my words held the smallest shred of truth.

"Of course you can. Where the hell's this even coming from?"

I closed my eyes, needing to see this through to the end. "I've already had the experiences you've yet to have. I don't want to hold you back. I want you to get your dream of playing in the pros. I want you to meet a girl you want to spend the rest of your life with." My stomach roiled at the vision of him in a tux and some beautiful girl beaming next to him at the altar. "I want you to buy your first house." It became more and more difficult to keep my voice steady and tears from spilling down my cheeks. "And I want you to fill that house with little kids because you're gonna make an amazing dad someday."

"Why are you telling me what I may think in the future? All I care about is how I feel right now. And right now, I can't get enough of you."

I forced my eyes to look at him. "It's for the best."

His face scrunched incredulously. "Whose best?"

"Before we get in any deeper."

He jumped to his feet, tunneling his fingers through his hair. "What the fuck, Marin?" he growled. "I'm already in deep. And so are you."

Ignoring his words—his accurate words, I trudged on. "Look. Right now, the only ones who'll be hurt are us." I averted my gaze, unable to bear the anger in his eyes or the splintering of my heart.

"CJ will be hurt, and you know it," he said through clenched teeth.

My eyes dropped to my lap, knowing what I needed to do. "I need someone who's going to be here for CJ. I thought my feelings for you were enough. But I have a little boy who needs a consistent man in his life."

His eyes narrowed. "What?"

"And even though you'll be back in May, it's only temporary. You're heading to the pros. You know it and I know it."

"So?"

"So, we're not following you around the country. CJ needs stability, more so now than ever."

"You knew when you asked me to hang out with him I'd be leaving. And when you decided to be with me, that was a risk you were willing to take. What the hell has changed?"

I couldn't even look at him. I hated what I was doing. I hated how I was hurting him. I hated how I was hurting me.

"I know this hurts right now because it's hurting me too. I care about you, Trace. So much." I tried to keep the quiver from my voice from breaking through, but it did. "But I can't have CJ hurt any more than he's already been hurt. And you and I can't keep carrying on like a couple of newlyweds. It's been fun. You reminded me what it's like to be happy again. To feel so cherished. To be wanted—"

He dropped to his knees in front of me and grabbed my hands. "Then don't do this. I can be here for him. I can be here for you."

I closed my eyes, dragging in a shaky breath. "I need to be the adult here. I need to be the voice of reason. Don't make this harder than it already is."

His grip tightened on mine. "You think I'm just gonna let you walk out of my life?"

"You're the one who's leaving."

"Don't. Don't use that. I'm three hours away."

"You have games on weekends. You can't be driving home when you have free time. I want you to enjoy school. Enjoy being a single guy with professional dreams. I don't want your obligation to me and CJ to hold you back. You'll end up resenting us and we don't want that."

He dropped my hands and stood up, glaring down at me. "I need to get outta here before I say something I'm gonna regret and I don't wanna do that."

I nodded, completely understanding that I'd blindsided him. I held back my tears until he'd walked out the door, slamming it behind him. Then I dropped to the floor and let them spill.

Trace

I stormed into my parents' kitchen, slamming the door behind me. Marin had gone and lost her fucking mind.

"Trace?"

Great.

My mother stepped into the kitchen, pushing her hoop earring into her ear looking ready for a night out with my dad. "I didn't know you were coming home."

I shrugged, though the anger had to be rolling off me in waves.

"Do you have plans with…"

"Stop! Just stop acting like you really want to know?"

She lifted a shoulder, feigning indifference. "You two have a fight?"

"You'd just love that, wouldn't you?"

"Don't act like I'm the bad guy here. I can't help if I feel like you're throwing everything away for some woman and her kid."

"For the last time, they have names."

My father stepped into the kitchen, his eyes taking in the tension clearly visible between my mother and me. "Trace. Good to see you." He walked over and gave me a hug.

"I'm just passing through," I explained, trying not to take my anger out on him.

"He's here to see them," my mother said.

Anger pulsed inside me. Not only had Marin gone and fucked everything up, but now I had to deal with my mother's shit.

"Trace. You're in college," she continued. "Do you plan on coming home every time the boy has a game? Or when she needs you to watch him while she runs errands? It's impractical to think it can work with you at school and her here. Why put the boy through this? Why put yourself through this?"

Her words were so eerily similar to Marin's. My eyes narrowed. "Did you talk to her?"

"What are you talking about?"

"That's exactly the shit she just fed me."

My mother's face lit up for a brief moment before she controlled it. "Well, she's smarter than I gave her credit for."

"Did you offer her money?"

"What?"

My stunned eyes shot to my father, looking for him to confirm what I already knew.

He shrugged. I should've known. He couldn't control my mother any more than I could.

My eyes shot back to my mother. "Did you threaten her?"

Her eyes rounded. "I can't believe you'd ask me something like that."

"Why not? She ended it out of nowhere. You have to be holding something over her."

She pressed her hand dramatically to her chest. "You give me a lot more credit than I deserve."

I shook my head, needing air. Needing to let off steam. Needing to punch a fucking wall. I turned and stormed out. I'd go back to Marin's and talk some sense into her. I'd make her see she was wrong. I could be there for her and CJ.

The only problem was when I rounded the corner to her house, her car was gone.

Marin

As soon as Gayle's front door opened, I walked into her opened arms, my tears streaming down my cheeks.

"I wanna kill him," she said.

"How is he still controlling me?"

"That's what men like him do." She squeezed me closer, allowing me to cry into her shoulder.

"I was so blind."

"Oh, honey. You thought you were in love. No one faults you for Charles being an asshole. There's gotta be something we can do to stop him," she said.

"There's nothing," I sniffled, wiping my runny nose on her shirt. "This is the only way."

"Can I at least slash his tires?"

"He'll probably think it was me."

"Not if I leave a note in spray paint across his windshield," she said.

I normally would have laughed at her crazy antics, but I physically couldn't. Charles had single-handedly destroyed everything good in my life, except my son. The son-of-a-bitch just couldn't let me be happy. "What did I do to deserve this?"

"Nothing. This is all him wanting to stay in control."

"But how long am I going to have to pay for marrying him?"

CHAPTER EIGHTEEN

Trace

"Dude. What's wrong with you?" Caden dropped down beside me on the sofa.

I was crushing another opponent in the video game I'd become obsessed with since getting dumped. It was the only thing that occupied my mind and stopped me from going fucking ballistic because Marin wasn't answering my calls or texts. The irony hadn't been lost on me that she thought I'd be the one to hurt her.

"You can pretend I'm not sitting here, but I know you can hear me. So, if you got some chick pregnant, I'm here if you need to talk."

My attention shot to him, my brows pinching together. "What?"

He shrugged. "It's the only thing I could think of that would make you walk around here like a zombie for the past week."

"On what planet does zombie equal getting a girl knocked up?"

"It's not just that. You haven't brought a single girl home since we've been back at school."

My attention returned to the game, in no mood to unload on him.

"Fine. Stay tight-lipped," Caden said, playing on his phone while I destroyed my opponent.

After a long stretch of silence, he said, "You're seriously not gonna tell me?"

I glanced to him, shooting him the universal glare for no.

"You having problems with...?" Caden's eyes dropped to the crotch of my basketball shorts.

I shoved him. "Fuck you."

He laughed. "There's the Forester we all know and love."

"I hate you."

Caden laughed as he jumped up and headed into the kitchen, returning with two beers. He handed me one.

I took the bottle and twisted off the cap and took a long swig. "Liquoring me up won't change the fact that you're not my type."

He laughed. "Hey, I've got no problem if you're—"

"I'm not."

He twisted the cap off his bottle and chugged. "Are you hurt?"

"Hurt?"

"Yeah. If you are, I won't say anything to Coach," he assured me.

"If I tell you will you leave me alone?"

His eyes widened, like he didn't actually think I'd cave.

"I hear Coach is benching our starting quarterback."

Caden paused, like he actually bought it for a second. Then he balked. "Real nice."

I flipped him off, focusing on destroying my opponent until I was too exhausted to keep my eyes open.

Marin

Charles pulled into my driveway at six. He knocked on the door, and when I pulled it open, he stepped inside, leaning in to kiss my cheek. I spun away quickly. If CJ wasn't there, I would've slugged him for such a stunt. He made my skin crawl. Every part of me hated him. Every part of me wanted to hurt him the way he hurt me and was *continuing* to hurt me.

He dropped down on the sofa beside CJ who was drawing. "What's going on, little man?"

"Hey, Dad."

"Whatcha drawing?"

"A football."

Charles' lips tightened as he stared down at the picture. "How's school going?"

"Good. My teacher made me the line leader."

"That's a great job." He glanced to me standing in the doorway. "How about you, Marin? How's school going?"

Could he not see the disgust on my face? Could he not see that I hated him for what he did and what he made me do? I smiled defiantly. "Great. I should've gone back years ago."

He lifted a brow—the same condescending brow I'd grown to despise. How had I forgotten that? "What do you say we grab some pizza?"

"Can we, Mom?" CJ asked.

"You two go," I said.

"Come on, Marin." Charles' tone reminded me what I gained to lose if I didn't play nice. "I want you to come with us."

"Come on, Mom."

I looked into CJ's hopeful eyes. He must've been ecstatic to have both his parents there with him. How could I refuse him? "Okay."

CJ and Charles jumped to their feet and walked to the door. I grabbed my handbag from the coffee table, noticing CJ's colorful drawing of a football. The words

To Trace were written in CJ's shaky kindergarten handwriting. I pulled in a deep breath and willed back the tears that clung to my eyes. I could do it. I could remain strong for my son.

I locked the house and approached Charles' car, grabbing the passenger door handle. I glanced up at the sound of a passing car.

Trace's mother drove by, staring with wide eyes.

Fan-freaking-tastic.

Trace

"I want you running an out pattern," Caden called in the huddle during practice.

I nodded as I stuck my mouth guard in and headed to the line of scrimmage. On the snap, I took off running, bypassing our defense. I easily nabbed his pass at the twenty-yard line, the ball dropping into my hands as I ran it into the end zone.

"Nice catch, Forester," Arnie said as I grabbed a bottle of water from Finlay on the sideline and dropped onto the bench.

"Thanks, Arnie."

"How's the little guy you brought out here this summer?"

"Good," I lied, feeling like an asshole for not knowing.

"He coming to the first home game?"

Seriously? "Oh, I don't know. Maybe."

"How about his mom? Now she was a looker," Arnie persisted.

What the hell? I didn't need reminding of what I'd lost at every turn. What I needed was to move the fuck on. "Well since he can't drive yet, they're kind of a package deal."

Arnie laughed. "She said you were just friends. But I could see it," he assured me. "I can always see it."

"Yeah, well, I've got charm," I said, standing and hoping to escape his inquisition.

"You? The girl's the one with charm. Don't mess it up."

You've got to be fucking kidding me.

What I really wanted to say was it had been the first time I'd been committed and what did I have to show for it? Not. A. Fucking. Thing.

My phone rang on my way out of the locker room after practice. *Mom* appeared on my screen. Great.

"Hey."

"I saw your friend yesterday."

"That's why you're calling? To tell me this?"

"She wasn't alone."

I could almost see her gloating on the other end. "Okay, I'll bite."

"Her husband was there."

I stopped and leaned against the building. "So?"

"So, the three of them were going out together."

"Again. Why are you telling me this?"

"Because I don't want you at school wondering if she's at home thinking about you. She's moving on. You can't fault her really. They share a child. It's in everyone's best interest if they reconcile and stay married."

"And you think that's what they're doing?"

"It would seem that way," she said.

And for the first time ever, I fell prey to her gossip. Because even I knew, it usually held a lot more truth than fiction.

Marin

I carried the heaping laundry basket upstairs, trying to be quiet while CJ slept in his room. I walked into my empty bedroom and placed the basket down on the chair in the corner, wanting to hold off until I wasn't so exhausted and emotionally drained. But it wouldn't get done that way.

I grabbed a couple shirts and walked to my dresser. My phone vibrated in my back pocket. I slipped it out only to find a text from Trace. Another one that would go unanswered. **Are you back with him?**

I couldn't believe it had actually taken Janine twenty-four hours to tell him. Her gossip skills must've been slipping.

I placed the phone down on the dresser and pulled open the top drawer. Trace's shirt, the one he'd let me keep, lay folded on top. I placed the other shirts down and reached for his. I didn't unfold it, just lifted it to my nose. His aloe scent still clung to the fabric. I knew the smell would eventually disappear, and all I'd have left of him was a T-shirt and the memories of the times we shared.

I blinked back tears as I dropped onto the edge of my bed, clutching his shirt to my chest.

If anyone could see me they'd think I'd lost my mind. And maybe I had. Or maybe I was just exhausted. Lonely. Sad. I'd been through hell with Charles and then this light—this shining light in the form of a college football player—entered my life and helped me see I controlled my happiness. Little did he know he was the cause of much of it. And with him gone, a dark cloud descended.

Tears trailed down my cheeks as I cried myself to sleep yet again with Trace's shirt in my arms.

Trace

I sat on the porch concealed by darkness. I watched the lightning bugs deep in the nearby trees. I'd taught CJ how to capture them in a jar. I couldn't believe he'd never done it before. That was one of the first things my dad had shown me that truly fascinated me when I was his age.

Fuuuuuck.

My brain was in constant battle with itself. One minute guilt flooded me, knowing I was on campus and not back home. Knowing if I'd only been able to stay, I still would've been part of Marin and CJ's lives. The next minute anger replaced the guilt, and I was pissed at Marin for ending it. She wouldn't even respond to my calls. And now I was getting information from my mother—the town gossip.

Was Marin back with her ex? Was she just too embarrassed to tell me after all the terrible things she'd revealed about him?

I shook my head trying to clear the clutter from my mind. I was Trace Forester. I wasn't some pussy who sat around brooding over a girl. I needed to get over it. I needed to figure my shit out.

The screen door beside me creaked open and Caden stepped outside. He leaned against the railing in front of me. "As your friend, I need you to tell me what's going on."

I glared up at him. "As *your* friend, go to hell."

"Dude, something's clearly up."

I shrugged.

"And as team captain—"

"*Co*-captain," I reminded him.

"Fine. As *co*-captain, if something's wrong with one of my players, I need to help fix it or find someone who can."

"Did you take that wisdom outta the captain handbook?"

His brows pushed together. "There's a handbook?"

I shook my head. "I appreciate you doing your *co*-captain duties, but nothing you say is gonna fix my shit."

His frustration with me shone in his entire face. "Well, let me ask you something. What would you do if the tables were reversed?"

I shrugged.

"I'll tell you what you'd do. You'd get involved like you did when me and Finlay broke up last year. You gave me your two cents and from what Finlay tells me, you gave her some advice, too. So, I'll ask again. What's going on with you?"

I dragged in a deep breath. I was exhausted. And bottling it up had gotten me nowhere. Avoiding Caden's eyes, I watched the lightning bugs flashing. "There's this girl back home."

"I knew it."

"She's not pregnant." My eyes cut to his. "At least right now she's not."

His forehead scrunched. "What's that mean?"

My eyes moved back to the lightning bugs. "She's got a kid."

"Oh."

"Yeah."

"Where's the baby daddy?"

I glanced to him. "First of all, he's five. Second, baby daddy? Where do you even come from?"

He laughed. "So, what's the problem?"

"She's almost thirty."

Actually saying it aloud, mixed with his silence, had me wondering if dating Marin had been a crazy thing after all. Had I been ignorant to the age difference since I wanted her so badly? Was being part of CJ's life an irresponsible mistake? Was what we were doing doomed from the start?

"I know what you're thinking."

"You have no idea what I'm thinking," Caden said. "If you like her, who cares?"

"She does. She broke it off."

Surprise filled his face. "Wow. She got Trace Forester to settle down and decided to end it?"

"She said she doesn't wanna hold me back. And she needs a constant presence in her son's life."

"Sounds like she's looking out for both of you. Can't really fault her for that."

"I don't. But she's not listening to fucking reason. And now I hear her ex has been sniffing around."

"Not much you can do about that. It's his kid."

A long silence passed. Now that I'd gone and talked about it, I felt myself becoming more frustrated, angry, and confused that she'd cut me off.

"What about her kid?" Caden asked. "Does he like you?"

"Like me? The kid idolizes me. That's who I was talking to in the bookstore."

"Have you spoken to him since…?"

My insides twisted. I hated that I hadn't spoken to him. And just as badly, I hated admitting that I'd let my little buddy down. I shook my head.

"Well, the Forester I know wouldn't give up. He rises to the occasion and loves a challenge."

"I'm no superhero, bro."

He scoffed. "That's for sure."

I laughed, something I hadn't done since getting kicked to the curb.

"If she won't let you be with her, at least don't let the kid down."

Caden's dad had abandoned him and his mom, just like the douchebag had with CJ and Marin. So, I trusted Caden when he told me what I already knew. No matter what was going on with Marin and me, I needed to stay in touch with CJ. He deserved that.

CHAPTER NINETEEN
OCTOBER

Marin

"Let me get it." CJ hopped down the front steps. I followed him to the mailbox, realizing it had been days since I'd last retrieved the mail. He pulled out the handful that had accumulated, dropping some of the envelopes to the grass beneath the mailbox.

I squatted and gathered what he'd dropped.

"I got mail," he screeched.

I stood up, pulling the envelope from his hand. "Let me see this." He was right. The envelope was addressed to him. The return address sent a chill rushing up my spine.

"Who's it from?" he asked, the excitement in his voice almost more than I could take.

"Why don't you open it and see for yourself." I ran my finger under the sealed flap and handed it back to him.

He dug inside the envelope and pulled out a piece of paper. Two slender cardboard rectangles fluttered to the ground.

I picked them up, staring down at two tickets to Alabama's next home game.

"Read it to me, Mom."

I took the paper from his small hand and read it aloud:

Hey Buddy.

I really miss you, but I know you're busy learning all sorts of cool stuff in kindergarten. I hope you've been practicing on my net. Next time I'm home I demand a rematch for our last game. I still can't believe you beat me! Oh, and I hope football is still going well. You'll need to fill me in on everything.

Listen, if you didn't notice, I sent two tickets for my next football game. I was hoping you and your mom could come and see me play. If you have plans, I understand, but I really want to see you.

Say hi to your mom for me. And I hope to see you both next Saturday.
Trace

I dropped the letter to my side and pulled in a shaky breath. I knew he still cared about CJ. A gesture like that just reaffirmed it. Reaffirmed I was keeping Trace away from someone who adored him. *Two people* who adored him.

CJ plucked the tickets from my hand and jumped around waving them over his head. "Can we go, Mom? Can we?"

It wasn't a question of *could* we go. It was could I handle going?

But was I really willing to keep CJ away from Trace in order to save my own heart? To appease Charles?

It seemed like an unnecessary risk, but also a no-brainer.

Trace

"Dude. You should go out there," I urged Caden from the high-top table where we sat. Finlay and her hot little roommate Sabrina had joined us at the bar, but then left us to dance.

Caden's eyes jumped from the dance floor to me. "Why?"

"Because some other guy is gonna think she's single and dance all up in her space." I took a swig of my beer. "And I'm in no mood to throw down tonight."

Caden shook his head. "I don't dance."

"That's not what Finlay said. She said you're a natural, especially when you go to that honky-tonk near her house."

He burst out laughing. "She said that?"

I nodded.

With a big dopey grin, he jumped down from his stool and wove through the bodies on the dance floor, stepping up behind Finlay and grabbing her hips. The look on her face when she thought some guy was feeling her up was priceless. But Caden quickly earned a smile from Finlay when she realized he had grabbed her. My gut clenched watching them. I hadn't realized how much I missed surprise smiles from Marin when I did something to elicit them.

Fuck that.

This night was about forgetting. Because I'd taken the high road and sent tickets and got nothing in return. Not a call. Not a text. Nothing.

I tipped back my beer and took a long swig. Why the hell hadn't she contacted me? She's the one who ended it. So why blow me off? Was she afraid of what would happen if she spoke to me? If I reminded her how good we were together?

On the dance floor, Finlay threw back her dark waves in laughter as Caden pulled her into him, dropping a kiss on her lips as they moved to the music. I averted my gaze, glancing around the crowded bar. Girls nearby were getting ready to swarm. I could tell in the way they got all giggly once I made eye contact. For some reason, once midnight hit, girls got gutsy, throwing themselves at me like I was something special because I played football. But right then, in a crowded bar at a table all alone, I was a sitting duck.

"Shameless."

My head twisted to my left. Sabrina had slipped onto the stool beside me, her cheeks flushed, her long blonde hair a halo of light in the otherwise dark bar. I knew from the times we'd hung out with Caden and Finlay that she wasn't a girl to throw herself at anybody. She was too hot for that. But I hadn't missed the way her hand brushed mine when she laughed at my jokes or the way she leaned into me if we were walking beside each other. My eyes narrowed on hers. "What?"

"The girls. They're shamelessly ogling you. Now if you enjoy that kind of attention—which I've heard you do, I can leave you alone and let the vultures descend. But if you're as scared as you look right now, well, I can sit here and keep them at bay."

"I'm not scared."

"Oh *sure*," Sabrina laughed. "I'm sure nothing scares you."

I took another long swig of my beer. "I didn't say *nothing* scares me. I just said *girls* don't scare me."

"Yeah, but there's a difference between girls and drunk girls."

"What's that?"

She smirked. "Drunk girls have no shame. And oftentimes no underwear."

I choked on my drink. "What makes you an expert?"

She lifted her shoulder. "I may have been one of those girls at one time."

"Panty-less?"

She cocked her head, but I could see she wanted to laugh. "If you want to pretend you're not scared of what might happen if I leave you alone…"

My eyes assessed her. She certainly had looks, but I wondered if she realized how amusing she was. I stuck out my hand. "Have we met? I'm Trace Forester."

I was just joking of course; we'd known each other for almost a year, when we met at the same bar. That night, some jerkoffs were harassing Sabrina and Finlay, and I'd come to their rescue. I'd also gotten her number but didn't call because I didn't want Finlay hating me for sleeping with her roommate.

Sabrina laughed as she extended her hand, going along with the charade. "Sabrina. Finlay's brilliant roommate and killer dancer."

I laughed. It had been some time since I'd laughed with a girl and meant it. "Well, Finlay's brilliant roommate and killer dancer, why don't we let these girls down easily and—" I ticked my head toward Caden and Finlay on the dance floor. "Show those two how it's done?"

She laughed as she hopped down from her stool. "I thought you'd never ask."

I placed my hand on the small of her back and led her out to the dance floor, elbowing Caden as we moved into the space beside him and Finlay. The music blared through the speakers above us making it easier to find my rhythm with Sabrina. I put my hands on her hips as she smiled up at me. Within minutes, she'd grabbed my hand and lifted it in the air, spinning herself under my arm, laughing as she did. Forget the girls watching *me*. The guys around the bar were focused on her and the way she moved her ass as she twirled around the dance floor. She turned to Finlay and grabbed her hand, ditching me to dance with her.

"Watch out for that one," Caden called over the music.

"I can handle her," I assured him.

He rolled his eyes as we moved closer to the girls, dancing behind them and showing off our best moves.

Eventually, a slow song replaced the dance music. Caden pulled Finlay into his arms, which left Sabrina looking to me. I held out my hand. She smiled as she stepped forward, wrapping her arms around my neck. Her small body was a stark contrast to my tall build but I made it work, pulling her close and moving to the music.

"See," she said, staring up at me as the colorful dance floor lights reflected off her face. "No vultures."

"I guess I have you to thank for that."

She flashed a smile that tightened my balls. She was definitely the type of girl I'd taken home in the past. The type who liked to have fun. The type who let me have fun with her.

I stared into her blue eyes, looking for a sign that what I was about to do was a very bad idea. That it was way too soon. That I shouldn't go for it. But I found nothing. I was a single college guy. I could do whatever the hell I wanted to do. And if I wanted to have fun with a single girl, then hell, I was going to.

I smiled, flashing the dimpled smile that made girls go home with me. But Sabrina seemed unaffected by it. I knew from Caden that she made guys work for it. And something told me it'd totally be worth it. "Sorry I never called."

"Are you?" she asked.

My smile grew as I stared down at this sassy girl and nodded. "Would it be all right if I called now?"

"Depends." She tilted her head. "Are you going to this time or just keep me on what I assume to be a list of girls you might call late night if you're lonely?"

I laughed, liking the confident way she carried herself, keeping guys like me in check. I lifted a brow. "Which would you prefer?"

She pondered my question as the music continued to fill the dance floor. "I'd prefer to wait to find out."

I stifled a grin. "Deal." Yep. Working for it.

Maybe I *was* ready to move on.

Maybe Marin's radio silence had pushed me to move on.

Maybe being there and dancing with Sabrina was the push I needed to get back out there. The one that said I'd get over my heart being crushed into a million tiny little pieces sooner than I thought.

CHAPTER TWENTY

Marin

We pulled into the stadium parking lot and followed the path the parking attendants directed us toward. CJ was practically bouncing out of his booster seat as I found our spot in the back of the crowded lot and turned off the ignition.

I closed my eyes for a long moment, inhaling a much-needed deep breath. I'd barely eaten all week. My stomach churned with nausea one minute then filled with anxious butterflies the next. Sure, I'd watched Trace's games on television, but being there, in seats he'd set aside for us, set my nerves on edge.

"You okay, Mom?"

My eyes snapped open. "Yep. Fine." I glanced over my shoulder at CJ. "Ready?" I laughed as his door flew open and he unbuckled himself. I met him at his open door, grabbed his hand, and we were off.

We fit in with the rest of the crowd hurrying toward the entrance in our Alabama T-shirts. I obviously didn't wear the shirt I'd made for Trace, not wanting him to read into it. Though, I highly doubted he cared what I did anymore. Remembering what he said about girls painting his number on their cheeks, I'd painted it on CJ's cheeks in white paint. I'd forgone the paint and opted for comfort, torn skinny jeans and flip-flops.

Once we stepped into the stadium, it was entirely different from the last time we'd been there. The once vacant seats were filled with a sea of red. The noise reverberated around the stadium creating an almost electric buzz. Thankfully, I'd brought earplugs for CJ. The noise was way too loud for his little ears to endure.

We found our usher standing at the start of our section and followed him down the steep concrete steps. Each time I thought he planned to stop to point us to our seats, he just kept descending until we'd stopped at the first row behind the bench. My stomach dipped at the sight of the players on the field, my eyes instantly searching for Trace's number eighty-two jersey. We'd definitely see him in those seats, and he'd undoubtedly see us.

I glanced around at all the anxious fans filling the massive stadium. Trace had been right about all the girls with his number painted on their cheeks. But he hadn't mentioned the signs with various messages to him. By the looks of it, you'd think he was already in the pros.

"There he is," CJ yelled, pointing out at the field.

Trace tossed the football with his quarterback and roommate, Caden Brooks. He looked so at home out there on the field. In his uniform. In his element. He caught a pass and when he pulled his arm back to throw the ball, his eyes snagged on us.

CJ jumped around, waving his arms in the air like a little maniac. I laughed at his excitement as Trace lifted his hand and waved, a smile spreading across his face. My body quivered as his eyes shifted to mine. I quickly leaned down and whispered something to CJ, anything to avert my gaze from Trace's.

Before long, the game began and Trace had an amazing first half. And even though he hadn't scored a touchdown, he already had eighty receiving yards, which was quite impressive. He looked so confident out there. The way he ran. The way he caught passes so effortlessly. The field was where he belonged. He was born to play football. That I could see clearly now.

At half time, CJ and I shared a huge container of popcorn. He was having so much fun, it was literally breaking my heart to know that could've been our life with Trace. That could've been our reality—if Charles hadn't interfered and Janine hadn't gotten into my head.

I glanced around at all the fans. All the pretty girls. Trace could have any one of them. And the notion turned my stomach.

I was doing the right thing. I just wished it didn't hurt so badly.

The second half of the game began, and within the first two minutes, Trace caught a thirty-yard pass and ran the remaining length of the field. CJ and I were on our feet with the rest of the crowd cheering as Trace dodged around his opponents and took it to the end zone for a touchdown. The stadium roared. But instead of spiking the ball in the end zone as we'd seen him do on television, he turned with the ball and ran toward the sideline. Ignoring everyone who approached to congratulate him, he headed directly toward us.

My eyes widened and my stomach dropped to my feet. Trace stopped in front of us, reaching up and handing CJ the ball. The fans around us cheered as I just about melted to my spot.

Beneath his helmet, Trace's eyes cut to mine and he winked before turning back to the field and celebrating with his teammates.

"Trace gave me the ball," CJ said, hugging the ball to his chest.

People around us patted CJ on the back. You'd have thought he'd won a million bucks given the way he beamed with pride over Trace's amazing gift. I didn't blame him. Trace had made him feel special—something Trace was so incredibly good at doing.

Trace

The play clock ticked down and the game ended with us kicking the shit out of Arkansas. Our offensive line looked good and made it easy for Caden to complete his passes, hence my nearly two-hundred-yard game. I wondered if CJ and Marin being there had anything to do with it.

I glanced to their seats on my way off the field. They were empty. Why hadn't they waited to talk to me? Didn't they realize I wanted to see them?

Ignoring reporters who wanted an interview, I rushed into the locker room, pulling my phone from my bag. Marin hadn't texted. *What the hell?* I sent off a text to her. **Thanks for bringing him.**

Marin's message popped up immediately. **Thanks for the tickets.**

Seeing her words gave me the same nervous excitement seeing her in the seats had. I didn't think I'd be affected. I didn't think I'd care. But I was thrown off balance by the sight of them. By the urge I felt to go to them. By the urge I felt to talk to them.

And what I also didn't expect was the way having them there motivated me. I wanted to give CJ a role model he could be proud of. It was the first time I wasn't concerned with crushing our opponent, breaking another school record, or just making myself look good out there. It was about CJ.

And don't get me started on Marin standing there in a Bama T-shirt. I'm not gonna lie. It gave me a sliver of hope she was there to see me and not just because I'd sent tickets. But deep down I knew she wasn't there for me. She was there so CJ could see me play. I needed to remember that. I needed to remember we were over.

I sent off another text. **Would've liked to see you guys.**

I watched the text box. No dots appeared. Was she already driving home? Was she in that much of a rush to be away from me? After a few pathetic minutes of willing her to text back, I tossed my phone into my bag and showered.

After my shower, I threw on a navy T-shirt and jeans and tossed my bag over my shoulder.

Finlay rushed by me like a bat out of hell and dragged Caden into the back room. The two of them clearly couldn't get enough of each other. But if Coach caught them hooking up in—

"I think I know why Forester hasn't called Sabrina," Finlay whispered.

My ears perked up as I moved closer to the door.

"I think I know his secret," she continued.

"Forester's got a secret?" Caden asked with a smile in his voice.

"Of course he does. There's a woman and kid waiting outside for him. It's the same kid he gave the ball to."

Holy shit. They waited.

"I think he's a *dad.*"

Caden choked on a laugh as I bolted out of the locker room, immediately spotting Marin and CJ leaning against the brick wall outside. CJ clutched the football I'd given him to his chest. If the proud look on his face didn't bring a grown man to tears, I don't know what did. As soon as he spotted me, he handed Marin the football and ran toward me, launching himself into my arms. "Whoa," I laughed, catching him into an embrace. "Hey, buddy."

He held onto me tightly, only pulling back enough to see my face. "Hi, Trace."

Marin walked toward us with a small smile on her face. She was trying not to be affected by me. By the connection CJ and I had. By the way she once felt about me. "Hi."

"Going for the element of surprise?" I asked with raised brows, trying to hide how badly I'd missed her.

"Was it a good one?"

There were so many things I wanted to say. Wanted to do now that she stood in front of me. But instead I shrugged. "It was okay."

She snickered and I wondered if she too was brought back to that night she showed up at my bar claiming the service was just okay.

"So, what'd you think of the game?" I asked, hating that I couldn't hug or kiss her.

"You did great," she said, minus the excitement she'd shown when we'd talk after my earlier games.

"Did you expect anything less?"

She rolled her eyes, but I could see my cockiness still amused her. "Thanks for giving him the ball."

I lowered CJ to his feet. He looked up at me with big excited eyes. "Yeah. Thanks for the ball, Trace. Some girl offered me a hundred bucks for it."

"Buddy, you should have given it to her. I would've given you another one."

CJ shrugged as he reclaimed the football from Marin. "I wanted this one."

My eyes shifted to Marin who wiped the corner of her eye.

I wanted to shake her. I wanted to tell her it didn't have to be like this. But I'd never had to force someone to want me. I wasn't about to start now.

"Well, we just wanted to say hello before we took off," Marin said, clearly trying to get away from me.

"Who do we have here?" I heard Finlay before I saw her. She stepped beside me and stuck her hand out to CJ. "Hi, I'm Finlay."

CJ shook her hand with rounded eyes, clearly smitten. Finlay was pretty in that girl-next-door way guys like Caden fell hard for. "I'm CJ."

She nodded to the football in his hands. "I see you got yourself a souvenir."

CJ nodded. "Yeah, Trace gave it to me."

Finlay's eyes shifted to mine. "That was really nice of him."

"Sorry, bro," Caden said as he stepped up beside me. "I tried to stop her."

Finlay looked to Marin. "And you must be CJ's mom."

"Marin."

"Forester got you guys some prime seats," Finlay said, her eyes moving between Marin and CJ.

"Yep. We could see everything," Marin said, trying to be polite when all she clearly wanted to do was get home.

Finlay looked back to CJ as she hitched her thumb over her shoulder. "This is Caden. He's the one who threw the ball to Forester."

CJ's eyes widened on Caden.

"You want me to sign the ball?" Caden asked him.

CJ nodded. "That would be awesome."

"Hey, don't forget who caught the ball and scored the touchdown," I added.

CJ smiled up at me. "You can sign it too, Trace."

Marin pulled a marker from her handbag and handed it to Caden.

He knelt down in front of CJ and signed the ball. "This signature is gonna be worth a lot of money someday," Caden teased, though he was probably right. He was a hell of a quarterback and he deserved every good thing that came his way.

"Not as much as mine will be worth," I added.

Caden rolled his eyes as he stood and handed the marker back to Marin. Knowing enough to get Finlay away before she did something crazy like invite them back to our house, Caden dropped his arm over Finlay's shoulders. "Let's go."

"It was nice meeting you CJ," Finlay said. "You too, Marin."

"You too," Marin and CJ said at the same time.

"See ya," Caden said as he turned Finlay away from them.

Marin looked to CJ as my friends disappeared around the corner. "You about ready?" she asked him.

"I didn't get to sign his ball yet," I said.

CJ smiled and held the ball out to me, knowing I'd bought us a few more minutes. I took the marker from Marin and signed *To the best kid I know. Trace #82.*

I handed the ball back to CJ who stared down at my words. "Thanks, Trace."

I wasn't sure he could read yet, and I hated that I didn't know things like that. Hated that I was now an outsider. I tried to ignore the lump forming in my throat, but I knew they'd be leaving. And I didn't want them to go. "You guys want to grab a bite to eat?" I asked, handing the marker to Marin.

She avoided my gaze as she tucked the marker into her handbag. "Oh, I don't—"

"Can we, Mom?"

Marin looked to me pleadingly.

But there was no way I was letting her out of it that easily. "Can we, Mom?" I teased.

Her eyes flared, but underneath I could see that spark of amusement I brought out in her. "Fine. A quick bite."

"Should we get burgers or—" My eyes locked on hers. "Ice cream?"

Her eyes shot wide as I laughed.

"Ice cream," CJ said as Marin said, "Burgers."

"Fine," I relented with a smirk. "Burgers it is. Maybe we can get ice cream after."

Marin cocked her head as she suppressed a smile. I loved that I could still get to her.

We walked to the closest burger joint on campus. CJ, a virtual buffer, walked between us. Inside, we sat in a window booth, me across from them. Between mouthfuls of burger, CJ told me all about school and the friends he made. Marin ate quietly while looking at her phone, giving CJ and me time to reconnect.

I'm not gonna lie. Having her there, but not really there, sucked. So did her excusing herself and stepping outside once she finished eating.

I watched through the window as she sat on a bench, talking on the phone. Who was on the other end? Was it her friend Gayle or CJ's dad? I considered pumping CJ for information. But not knowing was probably better.

"Mom's in college, too," CJ said.

"I know." My attention moved back to him. "Isn't that great?"

He nodded. "Yeah. She goes when I'm in school and studies when I go to bed."

"That's not an easy thing to do." I glanced back out the window at Marin. She was doing it. She was really doing it on her own. She said she'd get back on her own two feet, and she was. It just sucked that it was without me. "I hope you're being a good boy for her."

His little head bounced adamantly. "I am."

I held out my knuckles, bumping them to his. And as I stared across the table at this little kid who'd stolen my heart, it felt natural being there with him. Sharing a meal. Talking about everyday stuff. Marin said I needed to get married and have a kid of my own one day. But what was wrong with loving her kid? I know Marin wanted a consistent man in his life, but wasn't me loving him enough, regardless of where I was?

Marin returned once our plates were bare. "Come on, CJ. We've gotta head home."

"Aw, Mom," he said, standing from his chair like the awesome kid he was.

Marin draped her arm around his shoulder and pulled him into her. "Aw, Mom," she teased.

I laughed, loving their connection. "CJ told me you're doing well in school."

She shrugged. "It's not easy after being away from it for so long, but I'm figuring it out."

I stopped myself from reaching out and touching her, though my hands itched to. "That's great, Marin. Really great."

Her eyes flashed down uncomfortably, as if my pride in her was unwarranted. It wasn't. It took guts to get back on her own two feet.

"I'll be home for Thanksgiving," I said.

Marin forced a small smile. "Oh, that's nice. Your parents must miss you."

"I want to stop by."

She tilted her head, as if to ask me not to push my luck.

"To hang out with CJ," I explained.

"Yes," CJ said, punching his small fist into the air.

"Oh," Marin said. "Of course."

That's when I saw it. The disappointment I'd hoped to see on her face. And I'd take it. Because at least it was something.

Marin

My textbooks lay spread out all over the coffee table. I could barely concentrate on anything. Anything but the way Trace made CJ's year by giving him that football. Or the way the two of them got along so well. Or the way Trace made me feel so damn happy. And as hard as I'd fought to remain unfazed—or at least come across that way—everything about our time together had felt so familiar. So much like home. So right.

My phone vibrated on the table. I lifted a couple books to find where I'd covered it and smiled when I saw the name on the screen. "Hi," I whispered so not to wake CJ who was asleep upstairs.

"Was it as awesome up close as it was on TV?" Gayle asked.

I sat back and let the soft sofa cushions envelop me. "Better."

"Marin, you know he didn't just do it for CJ, right?"

"Stop."

"No. That's what best friends are for. To tell you the truth."

"Some would say I'm being a martyr."

She scoffed.

"Fine. It sounded better in my head."

"The announcers were wondering who the kid was," she said.

"He could've been any fan."

"Not the way Trace made a beeline right toward you guys. And if you're wondering, you looked hot."

I rolled my eyes as my mind wandered back to the feelings Trace elicited. The regret. The sadness. The love. "He took us to eat."

The silence on her end was her thinking what I already knew. Bad idea. "How was that?"

"How do you think?"

"Torture?" she guessed.

"That about sums it up."

"You think he still wants you?"

Though she couldn't see me, I shook my head. "We barely spoke. He probably hates me."

"He wouldn't hate you, Marin. Be confused by you, maybe, but he'd never hate you. Especially if he knew the real reason you broke it off with him."

"Yeah, well, he's not going to find out."

"What if I send him an anonymous text?" she asked.

"I already told you. If he confronts Charles, which I'm pretty sure he'd do, we both lose."

"Can I ask you something," Gayle said, treading lightly.

"Of course."

"How are you gonna feel when you find out he's dating someone?"

A knot formed in my stomach. The same one that had been there most of the day. So many times, I feared his phone would ring while he was with us. Feared he had someone waiting for him. Feared he'd tell me he was dating someone. Feared he'd moved on. "Terrible."

I thought finding out my husband had cheated on me had been the worst thing to ever happen to me. But nothing compared to the pain of pushing away someone I'd fallen head over heels in love with.

Once I'd hung up with Gayle, I sat for a long time. If I was doing the right thing, it shouldn't have felt so awful. It shouldn't have felt so wrong. Maybe Gayle was right. Maybe I needed to tell Trace. Explain what was really going on.

My finger hovered over the contacts icon on my phone for what felt like forever. Could I call him? Could I confide in him and beg him not to confront Charles? Not jeopardize me keeping my son? I pulled in a deep breath and released it slowly, moving my finger to the photos icon instead.

A picture of Trace and CJ appeared. I hadn't realized how many pictures I'd taken of the two of them until I began swiping through my pictures. Them playing catch, playing basketball, at a carnival, at the beach. I swiped again and a selfie of Trace and me, lying on my bed, filled the screen. Our heads were close, our smiles wide. I swiped again. Another photo of us, only this time Trace pressed his lips to my cheek. My smile said it all. I was falling hard for him. I swiped again. This time I kissed him back. My eyes were closed. I thought back to that moment. To my elation when we were together. I desperately wanted that again. I desperately wanted that again with Trace.

My phone vibrated in my hand. Jerry's name lit up my screen. The hair on my arms stood on end. Why was he calling so late? I lifted the phone to my ear. "Hey."

"Hi. I saw you on TV today." He didn't sound excited. Why didn't he sound excited?

"Yeah," I said wearily. "CJ got a football."

"Yeah, I saw. I'm sure Charles saw it too."

A cold chill rushed up my spine.

"I need you to do damage control," he said. "Before he does something rash. Because given the close-up on TV, it seemed like you and Trace were still together."

My heartbeat walloped as I disconnected the call.

I sat for a long time staring down at my phone. How had this happened to me? What had I ever done to make the universe turn on me? I met a man who was charming and smart. I fell in love with him. And then he changed. And then he changed me. I thought I was smart. I thought I was strong enough to stay true to who I was. But it happened. Charles happened. And now I was stuck.

I hit Charles' name in my contacts and lifted the phone to my ear.

Charles answered on the second ring.

"Hey," I said, trying to sound like calling him was the most natural thing in the world.

"Is everything okay?" he asked.

"Oh, yeah. I was just thinking maybe you'd like to meet me at CJ's game tomorrow."

"Oh," he said, like I'd caught him off guard—or he had a woman over and I'd interrupted. "Yeah. Okay."

"Great. The game's at noon."

"I'll pick you guys up at quarter of," he said, way too cheerily.

"He needs to be there half an hour early." *You'd know that if you ever showed up.*

"Oh. Okay. So, I guess I'll get you at eleven twenty-five."

"See you then," I said. I disconnected the call and my stomach roiled. How long was I going to have to appease him? How long could I be controlled by him? There had to be another way. There just had to be.

CHAPTER TWENTY-ONE

Marin

"Run!" I yelled like the crazy football-mom I'd become.

CJ charged down the field with the football clutched to the front of his red uniform with the number eighty-two on the back. He passed the fifteen-yard line. Then the ten. Then the five.

I jumped to my feet as he ran it into the end zone with his flag still intact. I wanted nothing more than to rush onto that field and sweep him up into my arms and tell him how very proud I was. Instead I watched as his teammates ran to the end zone to celebrate with him. Once the excitement died down around him, he spun and scanned the row of parents seated on the sideline. His eyes met mine and I gave him a huge smile and a thumbs-up. He returned my smile and thumbs-up, looking so proud—so excited.

The coach called them to the sideline and took the ball from CJ who didn't look like he wanted to release it.

"What'd I miss?" Charles asked as he slipped into the empty chair beside me. The same one he'd abandoned fifteen minutes before to take a work call.

I didn't bother looking at him. "CJ scored a touchdown."

"No shit?" Charles craned his neck, trying to catch CJ's eye, but CJ never once glanced his way.

"Hi, Charles." A woman I'd never seen before greeted him as she sat down on the bleachers behind us.

Charles turned to see who it was. "Sherry?" The excitement in his voice turned my stomach. He jumped up and approached her. "What are you doing here?"

It was shocking that the only emotion other than hate I felt for Charles was disappointment. And not even for me. For CJ. Charles had always been self-consumed. He'd always been more concerned with what he wanted than anything having to do with CJ and me. He'd done me a favor by cheating on me. I just wished he'd let me move on and not drag this thing out. We were never getting back together. His need for another female's attention when he was there with me just solidified that even more. The old Marin might've put up with him flirting with other women, brushing it off as him being friendly. The new Marin saw it for what it was and would never put up with it again.

On the sideline, CJ glanced over at me with a huge smile on his sweaty face, unfazed by his father who was busy flirting with some woman instead of watching him.

God, I loved that kid. He really was the center of my universe. And that's why when push came to shove, I'd do anything for him. Anything but get back together with his father.

* * *

The subtle chill of the unseasonably cool October air brushed against my face as I sat on my front steps. I needed a break from studying before it was time to pick up CJ from school.

My next door neighbor, Felicia, walked up my walkway. "Hey."

"Hey, stranger," I said.

She laughed, her smile as radiant as on her wedding day. "How is it that we live next door to one another and we haven't seen each other since my wedding?"

I laughed. "Well, maybe because you're a world traveler."

"I've been back for months."

"Then maybe it's because I have a kindergartener who needs a chauffeur to and from school and football *and* I'm back in school and got a job."

"No way. That's great. I guess I've missed a lot."

I nodded. "Yeah. I'm trying to do it all and it's not easy. But it's worth it."

"It definitely is," she said, before pausing. "So…is there anything else I missed? Anything else you want to tell me?"

My eyes cut to hers, my brows slanted. "What do you mean?"

"Oh, I don't know. Anything having to do with that hot football player we both know?"

My eyes glided away; even the mention of him hurt. "Not really."

"Not really?" she said, dropping down beside me on the steps. "That's all you've got to say?"

I pulled in a deep breath. "Okay. We kinda had a little thing."

She screeched. "You and Trace Forester?" She dropped her head back and moaned. "Oh my God! He's so damn hot."

"I know."

"I already told Seamus he's my hall pass."

I laughed, understanding the attraction. Everything about Trace was sexy. And Felicia had never seen him behind closed doors like I had.

"Obviously, the hall pass thing is null and void now that you two—" Her eyes narrowed. "Wait. You *had* a thing? As in past tense?"

I nodded.

"What happened?"

"He went back to school."

Disbelief shone in her eyes. "That *bastard*. Didn't he know what you'd been through?"

"That *bitch*. I'm the one who ended it."

Her jaw dropped. "Why?"

"He's still a teenager."

"So? You're only in your twenties," she countered.

"He has his whole life ahead of him."

"So?"

"He needs to experience life," I explained.

She cocked her head. "Come on, Marin. You don't sound even the least bit convincing."

I huffed my frustration before unloading all the craziness that was my life on her.

Trace

I lay on my bed watching game tapes for our upcoming game against Georgia, trying to focus on anything but Marin and CJ. Seeing them had thrown me off my game. I'd been trying to move on. Trying to find something other than football to fill the void of them being out of my life. Then they showed up and blew that all to hell.

A soft tapping came from my door.

"Yeah."

My door cracked open and Finlay peeked her head in. "Can I come in?"

"Sure." I sat up, turning off my tablet.

She moved toward my desk chair and sat on the edge of it since a few of my shirts hung on the back of it.

"What's up?"

She gnawed on her bottom lip. Oh, man. Something was up. "Last year outside the hotel in Mississippi, you gave me some advice."

I nodded, remembering the conversation. "My boy was being a stubborn ass."

"Well, from what Caden tells me, Marin's being just as stubborn."

My teeth ground together. "Remind me to never tell him anything again."

"He cares about you," she assured me.

"Doesn't mean I won't kick his ass for breaking the bro code."

"Bro code?" She rolled her eyes. "Sometimes, you guys are so lame."

I placed my tablet on the nightstand, avoiding her eyes while stewing at my roommate for running his mouth.

"You're a good guy, Forester," Finlay said, redirecting my thoughts. "You don't deserve to be hurt."

I shrugged. "I'm over it."

"That why you haven't called Sabrina?"

I glared across the room at her. "You want me screwing around with your friend? *Really?*"

She released a frustrated breath. "All I'm saying is you're clearly not over Marin. And it's obvious she's not over you either."

"Yeah, well, it was all her doing."

"But don't you get it? She's hurting. I could see it in the way she looked at you after the game. I'm sure she thought she was doing the right thing by putting you and her son first. But that wasn't someone happy with her decision. That was someone who was kicking herself."

"So?"

"So?" Finlay crossed her arms. "When Caden and I split up last year, it wasn't just him being stubborn, it was me being stubborn too. I could've easily explained that he was wrong about me. That his ex-girlfriend had fed him lies. But I let him believe the lies because I was too proud to admit I was hurt that he'd doubted me. He thought he knew me, and he didn't. Why should *I* have to explain?"

"I wasn't too proud to beg Marin not to end it, if that's what you're getting at."

"Did you tell her she broke your heart? Did you tell her you care about her? Did you tell her you'll be there for her and her son?"

I nodded. "Basically. It still didn't matter."

"Then maybe words aren't enough. Maybe you need to show her. Prove to her she was wrong. Prove to her that she and her son need you." Finlay stood and walked to my door, glancing back at me. "It might not happen overnight since you're here and they're not, but I'm willing to bet, she's not going anywhere."

* * *

I stepped onto the bus way too early in the morning with my headphones around my neck, ready for the four-and-a-half-hour bus ride to Georgia. We were the primetime game this week and would be playing under the lights. I slipped into a seat halfway down the aisle and shoved my backpack under my seat. Before I could slip my headphones on, my phone vibrated in my pocket.

My mother. Great.

"Hey," I said into the phone.

"Morning, honey. Getting ready for the trip?"

"Just got on the bus. What's up?"

"Oh, nothing. Just checking in. Wanted to wish you luck."

"You never call to wish me luck," I said.

"Well, your father and I will be watching."

"Okay," I said, skeptically.

"Oh, and…"

Yep. Here it comes.

"The boy's father is still over there quite a bit. I saw him just yesterday."

I stared down the aisle as Caden and Finlay made their way to the seats across from me. Caden lifted his chin at me before taking Finlay's backpack and stuffing it under the seat for her. He was always doing thoughtful things like that. He was definitely a better version of himself with Finlay in his life. I wondered if the same was true for me. Was I better with Marin than I was without her?

"Did you hear me?" my mother repeated.

"Yeah, I heard you. CJ's dad is over there. Thanks for telling me. I gotta go." I didn't even wait for her response before I disconnected the call.

It was as if she couldn't help herself. As soon as she had information she deemed important, she needed to share it. It was like a sickness. I liked to believe her telling me about Marin was because she didn't want to see me hurt. I just wished she realized she was hurting me by relaying the play by play of Marin's life when I wasn't there to do anything about it.

I slipped my headphones over my ears and closed my eyes, ready to get lost in my music. When I woke up, I had a job to do and I intended to wipe the field with Georgia.

Marin

"I won," Charles said, scooping the remaining chips from the pile on the dining room table. The bastard couldn't even let our five-year-old win. It was getting harder and harder to keep up the façade. Harder to not tell him what I really thought of him.

"All right, buddy. Time for bed," I said, saving CJ from another loss and wanting to get Charles out of my house so I could torture myself and watch Trace's game which had already begun.

CJ jumped up. "Okay."

I couldn't be sure, but he seemed as eager to get away from Charles as I was.

"Say good night to your dad."

CJ rounded the table and held up his fist to Charles to bump. "Good night."

Charles slapped his fist with his open palm. "Good night."

CJ looked to me, amused by the awkward fist bump before he hurried over and threw his little arms around me. "Good night."

"Head upstairs, brush your teeth, and then call me when you're done. I'll come tuck you in."

"Okay." And just like that, he ran upstairs and the bathroom faucet switched on.

I stood from the table and gathered the rest of the game pieces, folding up the board and stuffing everything into the rectangular box. Charles didn't move and it took everything in me not to walk to the door and hold it open until he took the hint.

"Ready, Mom," CJ called.

"Feel free to see yourself out," I said to Charles as I moved toward the stairs. "He'll probably ask me to read to him."

Charles shrugged. "That's all right. I can wait."

I cursed under my breath as I marched up the stairs.

When I walked into CJ's bedroom, he was tucked under his new sports-themed comforter. "Hey, buddy. You want me to read you a story?"

"That's okay, Mom. I'm pretty tired."

Shit.

I leaned down and pulled the blanket back enough to press my lips to his soft cheek. "You sure?"

"Uh, huh," he said.

"Well, I love you more than the universe."

"Love you too, Mom."

When I finally dragged myself downstairs, Charles had moved to the sofa. He held the remote and flipped through the channels. I stopped on the bottom stair and stared at him in my space. He no longer belonged there. He lost that right. And while I may have been allowing him in for CJ, I didn't have to put up with him when CJ was asleep.

"Hey," he smiled as he noticed me standing there.

"What are you doing?" I asked.

"Looking for something for us to watch."

The hair on the back of my neck prickled. Was he for real? Had he forgotten what he'd done to me? To our family? What he was *still* doing? God, he was delusional if he thought I was spending another minute with him. "That's not what I meant." I moved to the loveseat and sat, facing him with my elbows on my thighs and my hands wringing in front of me. If I didn't keep speaking, my nerves threatened to betray me. "I need you to stop what you're doing."

"What am I doing?"

"What you've been doing. I'm so sick of worrying about everything I do and say. I'm so sick of worrying that you'll take my son away. This is no way to live."

He stood and for a second I thought he was leaving, but he moved beside me. His scent instantly invaded my senses. It was spicy and dated and so him. "I've loved you since the first day I saw you." His hand landed on my thigh, his fingertips trailing softly over my jeans.

I stilled. Warning sirens bellowed in my head as my wide eyes dropped to his hand on me. He'd clearly gone and lost his mind. "You don't threaten people you love."

"Remember, that day at the café, Marin?" he continued, completely ignoring my words. "Remember our eyes meeting for the first time. We both felt it. That instant connection."

My entire face scrunched in disgust. "But now it's gone."

"You're wrong." He smiled, but everything about it felt forced and insincere—especially now that I'd seen him for the selfish, cheating, bully he was. "I've always wanted you. And you've always wanted me." He leaned forward, and had I not leapt from the loveseat, he would've kissed me.

"Are you crazy?!" I glared down at him, crossing my arms as if they'd somehow protect me from him. "I don't want you."

The lines around his eyes creased.

"I could never want someone who cheated on me then used my son to threaten me. Don't you think you've done enough?"

"We hit a bump in the road. Lots of marriages go through things like this."

I shook my head, trying to clear away the crazy. "This isn't a bump. This is the end."

"Says who?" His voice harshened.

"Says me."

His eyes flared, my unexpected nerve taking him aback and clearly pissing him off. "You sure about that?" he asked, his tone threatening.

"I've had it with your threats, Charles. And I've had it with you. Life happens." I threw my hands out to my sides. "And sometimes we just end up with the wrong people. It doesn't have to destroy us." I leveled him with my eyes. "Or make us do things we'll regret."

He said nothing, just stared at me with narrowed eyes that might have intimidated people in the courtroom, but all I saw was a pathetic man who ruined a good life.

"Go find someone who wants to stay home and have dinner on the table for you when you eventually get home. I'm not that person. I want my degree. I want to work. I want to feel fulfilled."

His jaw ticked.

"You need someone who'll cater to your needs and turn a blind eye when you stray."

"That happened once," he growled through clenched teeth.

"But that's the thing. I don't believe you. And I'll never believe you. I don't want to live like that." My pulse pounded in my temples as I trudged on. "I deserve someone I can trust. Someone who cares about me and only wants *me*."

"Like that kid?" he spat.

"This isn't about Trace."

Charles balked, and the way he did made me realize he'd never understand what *he'd* done. How could he not see that Trace had been a savior. Not his competition.

"Trace did nothing wrong. He was there for me when I needed someone. And deep down, I liked who I was with him. He reminded me who the real me was. Who the real me *is*."

Charles hands fisted at his sides, his cheeks flaming.

"Please don't take CJ away from me. I love him more than—"

"The universe?" he said, like it was something vulgar.

I nodded, tears sitting at the ready. "You may hate me, but do what's right for your son. You'll always be his dad."

He pushed himself to his feet. I braced myself, unsure what he'd do now that I'd stood up to him. He walked to the door, glancing back at me once he'd opened it.

I searched his eyes for compassion. Understanding. Regret. But found nothing.

"I hope you're ready for a battle," he said, before turning and walking out.

CHAPTER TWENTY-TWO
NOVEMBER

Trace

Music blared out of the speakers as I made my way unsteadily down the hallway. By the time midnight hit, I'd had way too much to drink. Half the school had shown up to my house to celebrate. And every time I turned around, someone handed me a shot.

A girl I'd hooked up with sophomore year gave me the same fuck me eyes she'd given me then. "Happy birthday, Forester."

"Thanks." I continued down the hall, using the wall for support.

"Happy birthday, Forester," a few others said in unison as I climbed the steps, needing to take a leak in my bathroom—off limits during parties.

Finlay and Caden's voices trickled into the hallway as I passed his room. Finlay wasn't crazy about crowds, so I appreciated Caden throwing me the party in the first place.

Caden's door swung open, and Finlay's sassy roommate Sabrina slipped out, her eyes rounding when she spotted me in the empty hallway. "Hey," she said, her hips swaying enticingly as she walked toward me. The look in her eyes told me she liked finding me all alone and drunk as hell. "What are you doing up here?" she asked, a big smile on her face.

"Escaping the crowd." *Oh, fuck.* I was slurring.

She laughed. "Yeah. I guess this is what it looks like to have half the campus at your house."

"What can I say? Kissing my teens goodbye is something to be celebrated." I ticked my head toward my closed door. "Wanna keep me company?"

One of her perfect brows arched. "You never called."

"And what would a girl like you have done if I had?"

She lifted her shoulder. "I guess you missed your chance to find out."

I motioned toward my room again. "So, you coming?"

"What if I say no?"

I opened my door, happy to find it unoccupied. "Then I guess you'll miss your chance to find out what my room really looks like."

"So, all of last year's Snapchats should be ignored?"

I laughed as she brushed by me and stepped inside my room. Her eyes took in my dark blue walls and big bed in the center of the room. I closed the door and locked us inside. She walked to my bed and dropped down onto the edge. I stood there staring at her, my vision a bit hazy, but not too hazy to realize how damn hot she was. And how fun she was. And how sassy she was.

Fuuuuck. Was I ready for this?

"I'll be right back," I said, bolting into my bathroom and pissing for a solid minute. Relieving myself felt so damn good. Would scratching my other itch with Sabrina feel as good? What was I saying? Of course it would.

I washed my hands and stared at my bloodshot eyes in the mirror. Was I that guy anymore? Could I sleep with her with no strings attached? I obviously wasn't looking for a relationship. Been there. Done that. It was an epic fail.

I turned to the door and reached for one of the two door handles playing tricks with my eyes. Somehow, I managed to grasp the actual handle and twist it. My phone buzzed in my pocket. I released the handle and slipped my phone out.

Welcome to your twenties.

Holy shit. I staggered back and dropped down onto the edge of the tub, staring down at the words on my phone. Should I respond? Should I make her wait? Should I ignore it the way she'd ignored my texts? *Fuck it.* My thumbs pounded away at the screen. **Is this a drunk text?**

Is there any other kind?

I laughed, picturing her snuggled up on her comfy sofa with a bottle of beer the douchebag wouldn't let her drink. Or better yet, in her bed with a bottle of whipped cream on her nightstand, just waiting to be used. **Well thx for remembering.**

There was a long pause. I knew I'd left Sabrina alone in my room, but I felt compelled to give Marin two more minutes. My heart bounced around in my chest. I didn't want to be excited. I didn't want to feel anything. I had a willing girl—at least I thought she was willing— in my room waiting for me. Another text popped up. **You off sowing your wild oats?**

I scoffed at the irony. **Was trying to. You just interrupted.**

There was another long pause.

Did I want her to think I'd moved on? Did I want to hurt her the way she'd hurt me? **I miss my little buddy.**

He misses you too.

I drew a deep breath and let my drunk-ass speak for me. **I miss my girl.**

There was a long pause before Marin's words popped up. **Enjoy your night, Trace.**

Disappointment filled me as I stared at her words. There was nothing more to say. She always seemed to have the last word. And for some reason, her last words always sucked.

A knock on the bathroom door sent my eyes jumping to it. "Forester? You okay in there?"

Fuck.

I shoved my phone into my pocket and stood from the tub, scrubbing my hands up and down my face. *Get it together and get her naked.* I opened the door to find Sabrina standing there looking all cute and willing. Her blonde hair reminded me of Marin's. The coy smile on her face made me see Marin's.

Shit. Fuck. Dammit.

I walked over to the foot of my bed and dropped down. "Come sit."

Sabrina hesitated, observing me as she stood there. I must've looked like a drunken mess as I patted the spot beside me. She walked over and sat.

I twisted to face her, inhaling the scent of something fruity. I was used to Marin's faint lavender scent. It always made being around her feel like home. *Fuck.* "I just got a text from someone I dated this summer."

Sabrina stared at me, confusion etched in her features. "Okay?"

"She broke it off once I got back here."

"Wow. I'm surprised *she* broke it off. You're not exactly known for monogamy."

"I didn't cheat on her if that's what you're thinking."

She shook her head. "Just stating the facts."

"Well, she's different."

She rolled her eyes. "Yes, we're all different. That's what makes things interesting."

"No. I mean she's older and she thinks she's holding me back." I left out the CJ part since I'd already admitted way more than I would've if I wasn't drunk off my ass.

Sabrina tipped her head. "Hate to state the obvious yet again, Forester, but she kinda just did hold you back."

"Bullshit," I said, calling her bluff.

She shrugged coyly. "I guess you'll never know."

I snickered. "Yeah, well I'm starting to think that's a good thing."

Stunned by my honesty, Sabrina shoved my arm. "Thanks a lot."

"No, I meant if we hooked up, we wouldn't be talking like this."

"Yeah," she sassed. "That's kinda the point."

I laughed. So did she. I liked Sabrina. I liked her enough not to let anything happen. "I want you as a friend."

"Said no guy to me ever."

I didn't doubt it. "Yeah, but now we can dance at the bar with no awkwardness hanging over us. And—"

"There's more?"

I smirked. "Just think how good I'll make you look out there."

"You're a conceited bastard," she said.

"It's a curse."

"And the more I get to know you, your cheesiness is kind of annoying. So, maybe you're right."

"I'm always right—wait. Did you call me cheesy?"

She rolled her eyes. She liked me. And I liked knowing she did. "So, what are you gonna do?" she asked.

Unable to sit upright any longer, I fell back onto my bed. "About what?"

Sabrina reclined beside me. "This girl. She's obviously still into you."

I turned my head to look at her. "What makes you say that?"

Her head fell toward mine. "She texted you as soon as your birthday hit. You said she's older. Maybe she was waiting for the dreaded *teen* to be dropped from your age."

Was she right? Was Marin waiting? Was she realizing CJ needed me in his life? Was she opening the door for us again?

Sabrina stared at me, watching my eyes closely. "You're clearly still into her, Forester. There's only one way to find out for sure if she's still into you."

CHAPTER TWENTY-THREE

Trace

As I pulled off the interstate and made my way toward my neighborhood, I questioned if I was making the right decision. I had no clue what I even planned to say. I just knew I needed to see with my own two eyes if Marin was having regrets.

The black sedan that had been driving in front of me pulled into Marin's driveway beside an unfamiliar red SUV. I slowed to a stop two houses away. The neighborhood was quiet for a Sunday afternoon. But my eyes still shot around, hoping no one saw me sitting there like a whacked-out stalker.

The douchebag stepped out of the sedan and strolled up the walkway. I tightened my grip on the steering wheel, my heart pounding in tandem with his footsteps as he moved to the front door.

Were they back together?

I breathed a small sigh of relief when he knocked on the door, clearly not having a key. The door swung open and CJ stood there smiling. His dad patted him on the top of the head, visibly too uncomfortable to hug his own son. *Douchebag.* What I assumed to be Marin's mother stepped into the doorway. She stepped back, welcoming him into their home. But where was Marin? Was she inside getting dinner started? Were they one big happy family again?

That was all I needed to see to know her call had been nothing but the obligatory birthday call.

Happy fucking birthday to me.

And even if I thought it was the hugest mistake in her life to get back with him, it was her mistake to make. I just wasn't gonna stick around to watch it happen. Once the door closed behind them, I reversed the hell out of there like the chump I clearly was.

I was about to drive past my parents' house when I slowed to a stop. If my mother knew I'd been in town on my birthday and hadn't stopped to see her, I would've never heard the end of it. Cursing, I pulled into the driveway.

"Trace? What are you doing home?" my mother asked as I walked into the kitchen where she and my dad were eating Sunday dinner. "Happy birthday."

"Thanks. Where's my cake?" I teased as I leaned down and kissed her cheek.

She laughed as she jumped up and grabbed me a plate, piling it with food. "I would've made one had I known you were coming home."

My dad smiled as I leaned down and hugged him. "Good to have you home, Trace. Happy birthday."

I pulled out a chair and dropped into it. "Thanks."

"So?" my mother persisted as she set the plate down in front of me and slipped back into her seat. "What brings you home?"

"Can't a guy just come home to see his parents?"

"So, you came to see *them*?" she said.

I shrugged. "It didn't matter. They had company."

"I'm sure they did," she said, like she already knew.

"I get it. He's there all the time. They're back together. Great."

"Tell him!" my father's stern voice silenced the room.

My wide eyes shot to him. I'd never heard him speak to my mother that way before. My eyes shifted to hers.

She tucked her lips. She didn't want to tell me. For once in her damn life she didn't want to gossip.

My heart began to race. What the hell did she know? "Tell me."

She stared at my father, huffing her frustration. "Fine." She looked to me. "Her ex has been blackmailing her."

I tilted my ear in her direction, hoping I'd heard her wrong. "Come again?"

She crossed her arms and leaned back in her chair. "According to Felicia, he was going to try to ruin your name by going to the press about your affair with a married woman. I guess he wanted you to suffer from bad publicity, knowing some teams wouldn't be interested in drafting you if you came with negative press."

"That son of a bitch." I shoved my chair back and jumped to my feet, my head spinning and my rage at its peak.

"Sit down," my mother demanded.

"Are you kidding me? I'm going over there."

"There's more," she said.

More? I slowly lowered myself back into the chair.

"He threatened to fight for physical custody of their son if she didn't end it with you."

My teeth ground together, the reality of her situation rushing at me all at once. "That's why she broke it off."

"She's been protecting you and her son," my father explained.

Holy. Shit. A sober laugh shot out of me as I looked at my mother. "You finally keep your mouth shut about something and it's something that affects me?" My voice rose. "I should have been the first person you told! What the hell is wrong with you?"

My mother straightened her spine and set her chin in place, as if she had every right to conceal the truth. "I didn't want you risking everything for her. I didn't want you to be her savior and not care about your career. Not care that your name could be ruined."

I scoffed at the ridiculousness. "I'm not scared of bad press. My skills speak for themselves. No team's gonna pass up a chance at having me because of who I date. Don't you watch the news? Haven't you seen what some athletes have done and they're still able to play?"

"But they're not my son," she said.

I sat for a long time, my mind reeling. Had our age difference never really been a factor? Had her saying she wanted someone consistent in CJ's life been a lie? Was everything Marin fed me only to protect me and CJ? "Was it so hard for you to let me be happy?" I asked my mother.

"It wasn't about happiness," she said. "It was about your future."

"Marin and CJ were my future. Don't you get that?"
She balked.

"Trace," my father interrupted. "All Marin's efforts were for naught. He's fighting for physical custody anyway."

"What?"

"I ran into her lawyer downtown yesterday. He mentioned the hell she's been going through."

"You didn't tell me that," my mother chided.

He glanced to her. "Even I know not to tell you everything." He looked back to me. "He said she's staying strong. And he thinks they've got a strong enough case to ensure she maintains custody."

"Why didn't you tell me?" I asked him.

"I just found out yesterday, and honestly? I know you, Trace. I know you would've barged over there and potentially made matters worse for her. Give her time. She's handled it this far on her own."

"Yeah, but that's the thing." I glared at my mother. "She shouldn't have had to handle it alone." I looked back to my father. "I should've been there."

My father nodded, understanding my frustration. "It takes a hell of a woman to protect her man. Or in this case, both of them. Just let her divorce go through. Let her win custody of her son. Then make her see that we Foresters don't go down without a fight."

* * *

I lay on my bed tossing a football above my head. I had a paper to write for sports medicine, but my head had been too fucked up since returning to campus to actually attempt it.

What was I supposed to do now that I knew why Marin really broke things off?

It was one thing to protect her son, but I was no good at sitting back and letting her protect me. My father was right. If I confronted Marin's ex, it could ruin everything she'd been doing to protect CJ. I'd been serious when I told my parents I didn't care about the press. Marin and I were both in our twenties now. Big fucking deal we started dating when I was nineteen and she was separated. Shit happens. But I wouldn't risk her losing CJ. He was her world.

But now I was starting to believe that there was a possibility that I just might've been part of her world, too.

* * *

I ran to the sideline on Saturday afternoon. It was a scorcher with the sun beating down on the field like it was August. And, had we not been playing another southern school, we would've had the advantage being used to the high temps even in November. The home crowd was exceptionally loud thanks to my back-to-back touchdowns that gave us an early lead.

Finlay tossed me a water bottle as I dropped onto the bench after my second touchdown. I thought my game would suck after learning the real reason I'd been dumped, but the exact opposite happened. I exploded out there. Maybe it was because I had a sliver of hope now. Maybe it was because I knew I didn't do anything wrong. Maybe it was because I knew Marin still cared about me.

By the fourth quarter, we were up by twenty-one and had possession of the ball. Caden called my favorite play. The one that would undoubtedly replay on *Sportscenter* all night long.

On the snap, I took off running to the forty-yard line, then I cut across the center of the field, causing Georgia's defensive backs to zigzag across the field to try to stop me. The ball came within sight, I leapt up, nabbed it with one hand, and took off running. It took nothing for me to outrun them, taking it into the end zone to the eruption of the crowd.

Man that felt good.

After my shower, I packed up my stuff and headed toward the locker room exit. When I passed Coach's office, he called me inside. He gestured to the chair in front of him. "Sit."

I sat.

"You looked good out there today."

I lifted a brow. "Are you saying there have been games I didn't look good?"

He shook his head, amused by my usual cockiness. He knew I did it to be funny. He was one of the few people who understood how much football meant to me and how seriously I took the game. "Are you heading over to the booster event?"

Shit. "That's tonight?"

He nodded.

"Is it mandatory that we go?"

He stared back at me, his eyes all the confirmation I needed.

"Fine."

"Look at it this way. The boosters are going to want to see the star of today's game," he said, knowing flattery would get him everywhere.

I laughed. "How long do I need to stay?"

"As long as it takes to shake all their hands and act like you want to be there. They do a lot for this team."

"I know, Coach. I'll be there."

* * *

My fucking hand was about to fall off. I'd shaken every hand in the place. And there were hundreds. To be honest, it wasn't so bad to be told repeatedly how amazing I was.

I stood in the corner of the room discussing the game with Graham Oliver, a booster who lived and breathed Alabama football. An older man approached us, his hand outstretched to me. "Phillip Caster."

"Nice to meet you, Sir," I said, shaking his hand as Graham excused himself.

"Those were some great catches today."

I shrugged. "All in a day's work."

He laughed. "So, where're you hoping to go in the draft?" he asked.

"First, of course."

He laughed again. "No, which team?"

I buried my hands in the pockets of my khaki dress pants. "It'd be an honor to play for any team in the league. Obviously, I wouldn't mind staying close to home, but in the end, I wanna go to the team that wants me and wants to win."

Amusement shone in his eyes. "Ever the diplomat. It's good you learned that early on. You're gonna need it to deal with the press."

I shrugged.

"I learned from my time in the courtroom—"

"You're a lawyer?"

He shook his head. "Judge."

"In Alabama?"

He grinned at my sudden intrigue. "Yes. You having legal troubles, son?"

"A friend of mine is."

"Anything I can do to help?" he asked.

"I sure hope so."

CHAPTER TWENTY-FOUR

Marin

Jerry and I sat on one side of the long wooden table in a small deliberation room at the courthouse. Charles and his two lawyers, one on either side of him, sat on the opposite side. They spoke to each other in whispers, as if strategizing. It was likely they were just trying to intimidate Jerry and me who sat there silently. I hadn't seen or spoken to Charles since that night in my living room. And once he somehow managed to rush our divorce proceedings, my parents served as our go between—which was fine by me.

I folded my hands on the table in front of me. They trembled so wildly I pulled them back and placed them in my lap. The future depended on whatever happened in that room. Whoever the judge sided with.

We all stood as the judge, a middle-aged man with gray hair, entered the room. I glanced to Charles and his lawyers, watching the shock play out across their faces.

Once we sat back down, Charles' lead counsel spoke. "Excuse me, your Honor, but I thought Judge Thompson was overseeing these proceedings."

The judge smiled, though I wondered what he really thought of being questioned. "Sorry to disappoint, but with Thanksgiving tomorrow, Judge Thompson left early to avoid all the holiday traffic. I hope that won't be a problem for you?"

Charles' lawyer shook his head, but I caught the worried look he gave Charles and the other lawyer.

The judge requested that we discuss the distribution of our assets first. Surprisingly, Jerry and Charles' lawyers were able to come to an agreement that everything would be split fairly between us. And, contingent upon the results of our custody dispute, Charles agreed to hold off selling the house until CJ finished school at the end of the year.

"Let's move onto the custody portion of these proceedings," the judge said.

Charles' lawyers presented their case first.

Sitting there listening to them point out every reason why I wasn't a fit parent crushed me, especially knowing that everything I did—every decision I made—was for CJ. Charles' lucrative salary and the fact that I hadn't had a job since I was in college didn't look good. I just hoped when Jerry had his chance to speak, he explained it was at Charles' urging that I stayed home. Charles' lawyers also argued that I'd introduced a new man into CJ's life so soon after his father left. They made sure to add that this "new man" was no longer in the picture and implied that I would continue to have a revolving door of men in my house which would be detrimental to my son.

Jerry presented our case next. He argued many points, including the late hours Charles worked. And unlike me, who had parents nearby to assist me, Charles' parents had just recently moved to Arizona and were unable to assist him. As a result, Charles would have to hire a stranger to care for CJ when he wasn't home—which was most of the time. Jerry also stressed that uprooting CJ from the only home he'd ever known would be *detrimental.* As would pulling him from school a quarter of the way through the year. I loved Jerry for playing up the fact that I was a graduate student who maintained a job, a household, and raised a child. That seemed to fare well in the judge's eyes, as he smiled and nodded at me while Jerry spoke. Jerry closed by bringing to light Charles' infidelity and the stipulations he'd set forth for me in his quest to separate me from Trace, using CJ as a pawn.

Once Jerry finished, I released a long breath and unclenched my fingers that had turned white from wringing. The future now sat in the hands of the judge. I just hoped he realized how much I loved my son and how much I needed him in my life.

The judge glanced between Charles and me. "These proceedings are never easy, and I appreciate you not parading a slew of witnesses in here to make this any more difficult than it already must be for you. When we get married, we never imagine it will end this way. And while you may have fallen out of love with one another, I can see you both love your son very much. Would you mind if I ask the two of you a few questions about him?"

Charles and I both shook our heads.

He looked to Charles first. "What does CJ like to do in his free time?"

I watched Charles search for an answer, one he clearly didn't know. "Play flag football."

The judge turned to me.

"Charles is right. He plays flag football, but he loves basketball, playing catch, and fishing. He's also a great little artist."

The judge glanced back to Charles. "And what kind of personality would you say he has?"

"He's shy," Charles said, almost before the words were out of the judge's mouth.

"Actually, he's the sweetest boy you'll ever meet. He's kind and compassionate and he loves to joke around. He's also really smart and can tell you all the state capitals in alphabetical order by state."

The judge looked back to Charles. "And why is it that you think you should have physical custody of CJ?"

"Because she isn't fit to raise him. Her extracurricular activities will get in the way."

The judge glanced to me with one of his eyebrows arched.

I ignored the rage bubbling inside me and spoke from my heart. "You asked why I want physical custody of my son. That's easy. Because I can't imagine living without him there with me every day. He adds light to a room simply by walking in it. You can't help but smile with him around." I blinked back the tears in my eyes. "I want to be there for every moment, big or small. I want to be the one with the band aid when he scrapes his knee. I want to be the one who laughs when he tells a silly story about what happened at school. I want to be on the receiving end of his hugs because he gives amazing hugs." I wiped the tears that now leaked out the sides of my eyes. "I want to love him more than anything in this universe because he deserves that."

The judge nodded. "Thank you both. I'm going to need some time to deliberate. Since the holiday's upon us, I don't want to drag this out for you. It shouldn't take long to come to a decision and complete the court order. Why don't you go get a bite to eat, and we'll reconvene at two." With that he stood.

We all jumped to our feet as he turned and exited the room.

Charles and his lawyers quickly filed out, leaving Jerry and me sitting there in the now silent room.

I looked to him. "So? What do you think?"

He shook his head. "I don't want to jinx us, but I think it went well. I think he could see how much you love CJ and how much of an asshole Charles is."

I only slightly allowed myself to believe it. "You think so?"

"Your answers were amazing."

"They were the truth," I said.

"I don't think there's any way he could believe Charles is the better parent for CJ."

Unexpectedly, the door opened and the judge stepped back inside the room, startling when he found us still sitting there. "Sorry," he said. "Just forgot something." He grabbed a folder from the table and turned to leave. But he didn't. He stopped and looked back at me. "I hear we have a friend in common."

"We do?" I asked.

He nodded. "Trace Forester."

My body stilled. "How do you know Trace?"

A small smile tipped his lips. "Let's just say I'm a big fan of his. Though I'd reckon he's an even bigger fan of yours." With that, he turned and walked out of the room. The click of the door closing behind him nearly echoed off the walls.

"Holy shit," Jerry whispered.

Holy shit was right.

* * *

Three hours later, I was a newly single woman and CJ's custodial parent. Charles would have him two weekends a month which, in all honesty, was probably more than he could handle without his parents there to help.

As I sat in the driver's seat of my car after signing the court documents, I was physically unable to start the engine. My arms and legs still trembled. As brave as I tried to be in that room, I had everything to lose. That knowledge wouldn't let me eat or sleep for the weeks leading up to the proceedings. Now that I'd won, I had no idea what to do with myself.

I glanced down at the text on my phone I'd sent to Trace. **Thank you.**

It remained unanswered.

CHAPTER TWENTY-FIVE
THANKSGIVING

Marin

The euphoria from the previous day still hadn't worn off as the remains of our Thanksgiving feast filled the table.

"I'm going to explode if I put one more thing in my mouth," my dad said, slouching back in his dining room chair.

"Marin, you outdid yourself," my mom added.

"Only the best for my three favorite people." I glanced to the sofa where CJ slept soundly. The food overload knocked him out.

The ringing of the doorbell grabbed our attention.

"You expecting someone?" my dad asked.

I shook my head as I stood, moving toward it warily. I had a slight idea who it could be, but since he still hadn't responded to my text, I couldn't be sure.

I pulled open the door. My stomach dipped as goosebumps scampered over my skin.

Trace stood there. His light blue button-down shirt mirrored his blue eyes. "Hey," he said as though I was the most welcome sight he'd seen in a long time.

I swallowed down my sudden nervousness. "Hi."

He opened his arms and stepped into me, catching me off guard in a hug. "Happy Thanksgiving."

I patted his back and quickly stepped back. Worst hug ever. "Happy Thanksgiving."

"You must be Trace," my dad's voice traveled over my shoulder. He stepped up beside me—saving me from the awkwardness I'd created—and extended his hand to Trace who shook it. "Good to meet you. Come on in and join us."

Trace brushed carefully by me and approached my mom still seated at the table. "Happy Thanksgiving."

"Same to you. We've heard a lot about you."

"Mom," I said under my breath.

"From CJ," she explained.

"Trace?" CJ's sleepy voice carried over from the sofa.

Trace spun around and walked over to him, fitting his big body in the small space beside him on the sofa. "Hey buddy, happy Thanksgiving."

CJ sat up and wrapped his arms tightly around Trace. I glanced to my parents who both wore the same sad smiles. It sucked that I'd kept them apart. Sucked that I was forced to. "Want to see my new room?"

"You went and got a new room while I've been gone?" Trace asked him.

"Sorry." CJ jumped up and pulled Trace up with him, leading him by hand toward the stairs.

Trace looked to me. "Is it okay?"

I nodded as he trailed up the stairs behind CJ.

"Let CJ come home with us," my mom whispered once they'd disappeared upstairs.

"What?"

"Oh, come on. It's obvious he came to see you, too," she whispered.

"That's not what this is."

"You two have some unresolved business," my dad added.

"What? You, too?"

My dad shrugged. "I learned never to argue with a woman who knows more than me."

My mom laughed as she leaned over and kissed his cheek. "You got that right."

Trace and CJ's footsteps echoed down the stairs.

"Hey, CJ. Go grab your backpack," my dad said. "You're staying with us tonight."

CJ threw his fists up over his head. "Woo hoo!"

Trace's gaze quickly shifted to mine. I spun away and grabbed a couple dishes from the table, carrying them into the kitchen and putting them on the table.

"Sit down, Trace," I heard my dad say. "Tell us about the season. You guys look great out there."

I moved to the sink and braced my hands on the counter, taking deep breaths. It was one thing for Trace to be away at school where I didn't have to see him, but having him in my house after almost three months—and fitting in like it was where he belonged—hurt my heart. My head. And my resolve.

Trace's raspy laugh filtered into the kitchen as he filled my dad in on the season. From what I could hear, his team had one regular season game left, a division championship, and a bowl game. Then, if things went their way, a national championship game.

Pulling in a deep breath, I turned and walked back into the dining room, reaching around everyone to grab more dishes.

Trace stood and picked up two platters. "Excuse me," he said to my parents before he followed me into the kitchen.

I pointed to the counter. "You can just put those down over there."

He moved behind me, brushing my arm with his as he placed them down. With my back to him at the sink, I closed my eyes, trying to rein in the barrage of emotions flooding me.

"We need to talk," Trace's soft whisper brushed against my ear.

"You never responded to my text."

"I wanted to talk to you in person."

I released a shaky breath.

"Scared?" Trace asked.

"Yes."

He slipped his hand into mine, his chest pressing softly to my back. God, I'd missed his touch. I felt myself leaning into it. Starved for it.

"Bye, Trace," CJ said.

Trace dropped my hand as we both spun around. CJ stood in the doorway with his enormous backpack on his back.

"See you, buddy. Let's hang out tomorrow."

"Okay," CJ beamed.

I hurried over to him. "You packed yourself?"

CJ's head bobbed. "I even packed my toothbrush."

I pulled him into a hug and pressed my lips to the top of his head. "I love you more than the universe."

He giggled. "I love *you* more than the universe." He looked to Trace. "And you're not so bad either."

Trace walked over and ruffled up the hair of the top of CJ's head. "You either."

I released CJ and he rushed toward my parents who were already by the front door wearing their jackets. Talk about subtlety.

I followed him to the door and hugged my dad. "I'll come by in the morning and get him."

"Sure. Whenever. And if I haven't said it enough, dinner was excellent." He released me and opened the door, guiding CJ out with him.

My mom turned and hugged me, whispering in my ear. "Good luck."

Luck? I needed more than luck to be alone with Trace.

Once the door closed behind them, my house sat eerily silent. I zoned in on the hum of the air moving through the vents, trying to ignore Trace's soft breathing somewhere nearby.

"Marin?"

Needing a few more seconds to come to terms with the fact that I was suddenly very alone with Trace, I turned slowly.

His head was cocked, his features etched with sadness. "I miss you so damn much."

I sucked in a quick breath, unprepared for his words and the wounded look on his face.

He moved toward me until I needed to tilt my head back to look up at him. "This has been killing me."

There were so many things I wanted to say, but there was one thing I needed to say. "I know what you did for me. And I have no idea how I can ever repay you. Thank you for getting me my son back."

He lifted his hands and gently cupped my cheeks, his eyes, now serious, riveting between mine. "You got your son back. And don't think I don't know what you did for *me*."

"I didn't want you brought into my mess."

"Your mess is my mess," he said. "Don't you get that?"

I closed my eyes, cursing my decision to keep the truth from him. I shouldn't have tried to handle it alone. I should've let him be my rock. I opened my eyes and stared back at him. "I didn't want you hurt."

"Do I look like I need protecting? Because from where I'm standing, all I need is you."

My eyes flashed down, unable to let myself believe this was happening. At my lowest point, I couldn't have ever imagined a scenario playing out where we'd be back in each other's lives. "I didn't want to be a distraction for you."

"Would you stop trying to keep me away?"

I met his gaze. "Why? It was just a matter of time before you would've realized I was more trouble than I was worth. You would've realized that you wanted all those experiences—all those firsts—I've already had. You would've realized you wanted your own family."

"You crazy girl," he growled, dropping his hands to my shoulders and his forehead to mine. "I do want those things. I want them with you."

"But—"

"This is where I belong," he said, the sincerity in his voice bringing ripples to my belly. "Where I'm happiest."

"What about the pros? You still need to get there."

"I plan to. With you and CJ right by my side."

My eyes stung with unshed tears. "Don't bring up CJ."

"Why not?"

"Because I might just fall in love with you."

His smile reached all the way up to his eyes. "Well that's good. Because I'm already in love with you."

Tears slipped down my cheeks.

"*And* CJ."

I choked on a sob. "You need to stop talking."

His face fell. "Why? I'm serious."

"That's exactly why."

That cocky grin I hadn't seen in some time pulled at his lips. "There's not a chance in hell I'm leaving without you admitting you're mine. I know what I want, Marin. That hasn't changed." He grabbed my cheeks between his massive hands and his lips crashed down on mine, moving possessively over them. I opened on a sigh and that was all it took. Trace's tongue plunged inside, stroking away at my mouth. My body arched into him, every part of me falling lax as he wrapped his arms around me. I could taste the salt of my tears on his lips as I wrapped my arms around his neck. As soon as I did—as soon as he knew I wasn't going to fight it—he dropped his hands to my ass, lifting me against him. I wrapped my legs around his hips, swallowing his groans as I shamelessly rubbed against the erection in his pants. God, I missed him.

Trace moved us into the kitchen, swiping the dishes off the table to the floor. Dishes crashed and utensils pinged, but it didn't matter. All that mattered was Trace and me in that moment.

He placed my butt on the edge of the table and tore my top up and off me, easing me back on my elbows. He stood back and stared at me, his eyes moving to my lacy black bra, searing in their intensity. He reached for the first few buttons on his shirt and slid them through the slots, then reached behind his head and pulled off his shirt. Football had gotten him in even better shape. Every muscle and every dip in his chest was well defined.

I took him in. I relished in the sight of him back in my house, staring at me like I was the prize he'd been longing for. My pulse thrashed and my breaths dragged in and out harshly. I wanted him. God, did I want him.

"Is this one of your fantasies?" My voice was heavy with need.

His tongue shot out, swiping along his bottom lip. "Absolutely."

"So, what happens next?" I could not believe I had the nerve to ask.

His eyes heated. "You reach for the button on your pants and slip them off."

I reached for my button. "Like this?"

He nodded, his eyes zoned in on my fingers unfastening my button.

I pushed my pants down my legs until they dropped to the floor. I leaned back on my elbows in my bra and matching panties. "Now what?"

I watched him swallow, his Adam's apple dipping as he did. "You unsnap your bra."

My heart was moving so quickly it was a wonder it hadn't jumped right out of my chest. But I wanted Trace. And I loved in that moment that I could give him this. That I could make his fantasy a reality. I reached behind my back and unclasped my bra. The straps loosened and my bra fell forward. I watched him watch me as I pulled it off and tossed it to the floor. He'd seen me naked before, but never had he looked at me with such wanton need as he was right then. As nerves shook my body, I stared at him, waiting for him to look me in the eyes. "Now what?"

His eyes lifted to mine. I could see the heavy rising and falling of his chest. "Now, you unbutton my pants." He slipped off his shoes and socks, making sure to avoid the mess on the floor, and stepped closer to me.

My eyes dropped to his crotch as I sat up, reaching for his button and pushing it through the slot, carefully lowering his zipper over his strained erection. I slipped my hands around his hips, my fingers slid inside his boxers, guiding them down his legs with his pants.

A naked Trace was a beautiful sight. And a naked Trace standing in my freaking kitchen was even better. He pushed his clothes and some rogue utensils to the side with his bare foot.

"Now what?" I asked.

He smirked. "Now I fuck you in every room in this house."

My stomach dipped, the notion dazing me stupid.

Trace stepped to me. His hands braced on the surface of the table beside my panties as his bare skin covered mine. His aloe scent strangled me with desire as his lips hovered over mine. "Are you wet for me, Marin?"

Unable to take my eyes off his, I nodded.

"Have you been thinking about this moment like I have?"

I nodded, entranced by the control in his voice.

"Will you let me be rough with you tonight?"

"Will you stop talking?"

A smile broke out across his face as he captured my mouth with his. And as I wrapped my arms around him and he lowered my back onto the cool surface of the table, all was right again. At least for the night.

* * *

Rain pinged off the roof, waking me from the best sleep I'd had since Trace had gone back to school. My body remained tangled with his in my bed, the last spot I remembered him taking me before passing out from exhaustion. He may have been only a few months older, but I forgot the stamina a guy in his early twenties had. Props for me for keeping up.

"Stop thinking," Trace's sleepy voice warned. "We've got plenty of time to figure things out."

"Don't tell me what to do."

"Why? You liked it last night."

I snickered. I totally had. Every dirty minute of it.

He tightened his arms around me, the warmth of his naked body enveloping me. "I don't want to go back to school."

I could feel his steady heartbeat against my back. "Well, you need to."

"Says who?"

"Says every one of your fans who wants to see you kick Mississippi's ass tomorrow."

He laughed and his chest bounced off my back. "I'll score three touchdowns for you."

"I don't doubt it."

"Ever think of transferring schools?" he asked.

"To your school?"

"Yeah."

"A three-hour commute is a little far."

"What if I gave you a reason to move?"

I pulled in a deep breath as I turned in his arms so I could look him in the eyes. "Trace."

"Marin," he teased.

All I wanted to do was kiss him and never let him go, but the truth remained. He was still leaving.

"Say it," Trace said.

"Say what?"

He rolled me onto my back, pinning me beneath him. "What you're thinking."

"That you're leaving."

"Then tell me what you want."

"What I want?" I asked.

"What. You. Want. You got your son. Now what else do you want?"

"I want…" I stared up into his droopy morning eyes, wanting nothing more than to stare into those eyes every morning for the rest of my life. He'd helped me in so many ways. And while I thought I was the one fighting for CJ and Trace, Trace was doing the same thing for CJ and me. "I want chocolate ice cream," I finally said.

He smiled.

"And I want…" My eyes drifted from his. "Whipped cream."

He growled his frustration.

"And I want…"

He dropped his mouth to mine, pressing a coaxing kiss to my lips. One that was sure to elicit the correct answer. One that reminded me of everything we shared. Everything we'd done for one another. Everything we had to look forward to. When he pulled back, he gazed down at me expectantly.

I relented on a sigh. "A superstar wide receiver."

He quirked his brow. "Just any superstar receiver?"

I shook my head, stifling the smile that threatened to break loose. "Just one."

"I like where this is going."

"Me, too," I said, before kissing him with everything I had.

EPILOGUE
Two Years Later

Marin

"If it's a girl, I hope she looks like you," Trace said, holding my hand as the epidural began to work its magic and those damn contractions became a thing of the past. "Now if it's a boy—"

"He better have your dimples," I said.

Trace smiled, and God did I love him. Between our soon-to-arrive baby and CJ, it's all Trace ever talked about. I'm sure the guys on his team wanted to kill him.

My doctor entered the delivery room, stretching his rubber gloves over his hands as he approached. "How are you doing, Marin?"

"I feel ready."

"I bet you do." His eyes flicked to the television on the wall we hadn't bothered to turn on. "Hey, Trace. Feel free to put the game on."

"I'm all set," Trace said.

The lines in the doctor's forehead deepened. "But your team's playing."

Trace shook his head, his eyes returning to mine. "My team's right here."

Even after a year of marriage and drugs numbing half my body, my belly still quivered at his words. At the look he gave me with his pretty blue eyes I hoped our baby had. At the way he loved me fiercely and completely. At the way he loved my son and our unborn child.

As if he could hear my thoughts, Trace leaned over and pressed his lips to mine, the familiar zing traveling right to my heart.

"I love you," I said, knowing the words weren't even close to adequate for how I felt about him.

"I love you more," he said, wearing that dimpled grin I loved so much.

"More than the universe?" I asked.

"More than anything," he assured me.

I smiled as the doctor moved to the foot of the delivery table and examined me under the sheet.

"Looks like your baby's ready." He pulled over a rolling stool and sat at the end of the table. "You ready to start pushing?"

Trace and I looked to each other, wide eyed with excitement. He squeezed my hand tightly as the doctor counted to three and I pushed as hard as I could. I was so happy I could give Trace this. So happy his mother had been wrong. He didn't need some young girl to give him all the things he'd yet to experience. He just needed me.

"Good job," my doctor encouraged.

I thought back to the draft. To Trace going second. To him beginning his football career in New Orleans while I finished my degree in Alabama. To Trace's mother eventually realizing *I* was what was best for her son. I loved him before the money. Before the success. And given the way she started fawning all over me and CJ while he was away and I was pregnant with her first grandchild, you'd have thought our turbulent past had never occurred.

Life certainly had a funny way of throwing things off its axis. And while Trace's parents waited with CJ and my parents in the waiting room, it became abundantly clear that we had the support and love of everyone around us. And no one could deny we were in love. Because if it wasn't for Trace Forester, I wouldn't know what real love was. I wouldn't know what it was like to have a real father for my child. I wouldn't know what it felt like to trust someone wholeheartedly again.

"Okay," the doctor said. "Give me another push like the last."

I squeezed Trace's hand as tightly as I could when the doctor counted to three and I pushed.

"Good job, baby. You're doing great." Trace dropped kisses all over my face. "God, I love you so much."

I smiled through the pain because I knew he meant it. Knew he meant everything he said. Because from the moment we met (again), he had been nothing but honest with everything he said and did. And one thing was for certain, I could now see life through Trace's eyes. And it was a pretty sweet life.

"One more push and your baby will be here," the doctor assured us.

"One more?" I asked, shocked by the minimal pain and ease of this delivery. CJ damn near split me in two. At least that's what it felt like.

"I can see the head," he assured me.

I looked to Trace. His face held a mixture of love and excitement. "You got this."

Tears glazed my eyes as I nodded at my husband, squeezing his hand as I pushed again, this time giving it all I had.

The doctor was right. That's all it took. That was the push that brought our child into the world.

"It's a boy!" the doctor announced.

I looked to Trace only to find tears rolling down his cheeks and a giant smile stretched across his lips as they cleaned our baby boy.

"Thank you," he said, staring at the little miracle we'd made together as he stayed beside me still gripping my hand.

I lifted my fingers to his cheeks, lightly brushing away his tears. "For giving you a boy?"

He glanced back to me. "For making every one of my dreams come true."

"What about your fantasies?" I asked as the nurse grabbed for the scissors so Trace could cut the cord.

"Oh, babe," he said before pressing his lips to mine. "The second you let me into your life, my fantasies came true."

The End

OTHER TITLES BY J. NATHAN

For You Standalone Series
For Finlay (Book #1 Caden & Finlay's Story)
For Crosby (Book #3 Sabrina's Story)
For Emery (Book #4 Grady's Story)

Savage Beasts Rock Star Standalone Series
Kozart
Treyton

Standalones
Seren
Something About You
I Just Need You
You're the Reason
Until Alex
Since Drew
Before Hadley

ACKNOWLEDGEMENTS

Thank you to every reader who took the time to read Trace and Marin's story. I hope you enjoyed their story as much as I enjoyed writing it!

To all the bloggers and readers who have continued to spread the word about my books. I would not be motivated to keep doing what I love without you! Thank you so much!!!!

To my wonderful beta readers: Dali, Kat, Neilliza, Suzanne, Megan D, Renee Mc, and Kim. Thank you for taking the time to give me feedback. I value your opinions and ideas tremendously and appreciate your assistance. I am so lucky to have you all!

To my editor Stephanie Elliot. Thank you for always being there to make my books the best they can possibly be and for answering all my questions. Knowing I can depend on you has been a true blessing!

To Lindee Robinson for the beautiful photos of Jeff and Becca. I just love this cover photo.

To Letitia at RBA Designs for creating another beautiful cover for me. I always know you'll come through with exactly what I envision. Thank you a hundred times over! You are always a true pleasure to work with.

And last, but certainly not least, to my husband and son. Thank you for understanding when my computer is in front of me, or I just need a little time to myself. Please know I try to devote my attention to all my loves and desperately hope I'm pulling it off.

ABOUT THE AUTHOR

J. Nathan resides on the east coast with her husband and seven-year-old son. She is an avid reader of all things romance. Happy endings are a must. Alpha males with chips on their shoulders are an added bonus. When she's not curled up with a good book, she can be found spending time with family and friends and working on her next novel.